THE SPREAD

A ZOMBIE SHORT STORY COLLECTION

By Michelle Kilmer and Rebecca Hansen

Edited by Kevin D. Looney

ISBN: 0988252252
ISBN-13: 978-0-9882522-5-7

Dedicated to our mother, Victoria.

She has survived so much in her life we are certain she **would** survive the zombie apocalypse.

Mom, thank you for everything you do and continue to do for your girls.

TABLE OF CONTENTS

THE SPREAD

A ZOMBIE SHORT STORY COLLECTION

- THE ISLAND -

Michelle Kilmer and Rebecca Hansen

RUNNING ON FUMES

Gordon Kinder was ready to get back to Bellevue. He never felt right outside of the city, but was often sent out of town on business, spending more nights in hotel rooms than in his own home.

He had only been on Orcas Island for a few days and hadn't been too happy; especially to find when he'd first arrived that his hotel overlooked the water near the ferry dock. The smell of seawater made him nauseous and he preferred the noise of the expanding city to squawking seagulls.

After finishing a late morning meeting, Gordon had found himself in a local dive bar across the street from his hotel. It wasn't the nicest place around but any place that served alcohol suited him just fine. A few drinks in and Gordon had started eaves dropping on a few locals chatting with the waitress behind the bar. It wasn't long before he added himself to the conversation

"Hey, what's that you're saying?" Gordon asked as he rose from his table by the window and approached the men at the bar, "Something about a possible quarantine?"

He wasn't sure if he had heard them correctly, but had no qualms about interjecting.

"Oh, uh…well, my brother called me from the airport you see…uh and he's a mechanic over there and he said they got a real sick man who flew in from Lopez and that it's gone to shit, said they were getting ready to shut it down."

"What do you mean a *sick* man?"

"Well, I don't know sir. My brother didn't say much and I wasn't able to get any more information from him before the call cut off. Pro'lly just the old telephone lines on the island," the man said as his words faded, his eyes now looking through the bottom of an empty beer mug.

Gordon's mind raced. *What was wrong with that man* he thought? *Why would they shut down an island?* Just the idea of being stuck somewhere so different and outside of his true comfort zone sent shivers down his spine. After only fifteen minutes he left the bar, packed, checked out of his hotel and started making his way to the ferry.

As his car crept closer to the ticket booth, he noticed the ever-growing line behind him. *Just in time* he thought, *beat the crowd.*

"One ticket to Anacortes," Gordon told the man in the tollbooth.

"Might be best to get off the islands, I hear Lopez is having trouble," the man said.

Uninterested in making small talk, Gordon nodded, grabbed the ticket and proceeded to his spot in line. It wasn't long after placing his car in park that they had unloaded the awaiting ferry and starting directing cars back on. Only moments after the boat had left the dock the captain made an announcement over the loud speaker.

"Good Morning Folks, this is your captain speaking, we have just been informed that this is the last ferry to leave Orcas as quarantine has been issued on the island. We have been instructed that the discharge in Anacortes will take a bit longer than usual. There will be vehicle checks on all occupants to clear all passengers before you disembark. Thank you and have a wonderful day."

It seemed odd to Gordon that the captain was so calm about a quarantine, but he felt assured that he had nothing to worry about and was happy knowing he had made it off the island. The trip across the water took the expected forty-five minutes and the 'vehicle checks', if that's what you could call them, barely disturbed the boats offload.

He followed behind an economy van towing an airstream trailer; it had reminded him of the simpler times in his childhood, bringing back many fond memories. Those faded once he realized that the vehicle had no intention of going any faster than thirty miles per hour and he had no room to get around them. The van's exhaust traveled underneath the trailer and directly into the vents of his BMW.

"Come on, come on," Gordon yelled, as he coughed and pressed on the car horn. "We aren't on the island any more, pick up the pace!" His hand spent more time on the horn than not as he drove behind the trailer. It had been like this since they exited the ferry some thirty-minutes earlier.

The single lane road finally opened up and the first chance Gordon saw he signaled left and pulled alongside to pass, glancing quickly at the family inside. They had Kansas plates and must have been camping on the island, the man behind the wheel looked like he hadn't had a real shower or shave in weeks but appeared quite happy singing with his children who were bouncing around in the back seat. Gordon also noticed who he assumed to be the mother of the kids and the driver's wife looking somewhat unwell in the front passenger seat. She wasn't singing along with everyone else.

A punch of the gas and a hard right and he was in front of the van. He felt it necessary to make up for lost time by turning the passing trees into a blur of green along both sides of the roadway. At this pace he felt sure he would get to Bellevue in less than two hours. In the rear-view mirror he noticed the trailer towing van pull off into a KOA, the big yellow and red sign had created a break in the trees along the interstate.

Gordon looked back ahead just in time to notice his vehicle had veered off course and was headed straight into a girl walking along the side of the road. He swerved to avoid hitting her, causing his vehicle to overturn and barrel roll into the grass on the shoulder. The force of the roll sent Gordon flying through the windshield of his car and directly into the trunk of a tree.

"Oh my God!" the girl screamed, running to his aid. His body was a crumpled mess of broken bones and deep cuts. Ella had no idea where to begin trying to help him. She pushed a hand into a cut on his belly to try to stop the bleeding but instead she was cut herself on a piece of glass lodged in the wound. "Fuck!" she yelled, pressing her bleeding hand into her leg. She pulled her cellphone from her purse and called for help.

"There's a man and I think he is dying. He crashed. Yes, I'll stay on the line."

Michelle Kilmer and Rebecca Hansen

ONE WAY TRIP

"What do you know about the virus?" a reporter asked Brett McKay as he sipped horrid coffee in the Anacortes ferry terminal. Little more than a few small rooms, like portables strung together, the building was poorly heated and provided few options to escape the insatiable media. Brett avoided answering by scooting down the hardwood bench he shared with the man.

"Is it true, about the plane crash?" the reporter continued, leaning forward slightly in an attempt to catch Brett's eyes. Brett stood up and walked to a rotating rack of old paperbacks and, though he wasn't keen on fiction, picked one and started to skim read the middle of it.

"Look, I know you have clearance. They wouldn't let you on this boat if you didn't. So you can stop pretending like you don't know anything," the reporter shot at Brett, who returned the paperback to its dusty home on the spindle and reclaimed his seat on the bench. He could get his answers from someone else but Brett wasn't going to let the paper shark off easily.

"I know a lot actually," Brett turned to the journalist and smiled. "This coffee sucks, for one. I didn't brush my teeth this morning, which means I have horrible morning breath," he leaned into the reporter's personal space and breathed heavily on him, "and I know that you *don't* have clearance. So unless you want to write about this lackluster latte or whether I packed my toothbrush, you can bother someone else." Before the reporter could respond Brett left him on the bench and returned to his vehicle.

Outside, a light snow started to fall. The terminal, which was usually crowded but quiet, was a bustle of worried activity. Only twelve vehicles were permitted on the final ferry out, Brett's being the fifth in line, but there were over one hundred more stacking up behind the traffic cones that separated those with clearance and those without. Even though the temperature was several degrees below freezing, most everyone stood outside the warmth of their cars, waiting for answers.

Brett had just closed the driver's side door when, out on the water, a ferry broke through the snowfall. A wave of tense excitement rippled through those waiting for word of the fate of their loved ones. As the boat grew closer, those near the front of the expectant crowd could see that it carried no vehicles. Their excitement changed to confusion and anger. Shouting voices rang out but were silenced when a man's voice started talking over a PA system. Brett turned the ignition over just enough to roll down his window.

"Ladies and gentleman," the man calmly started, "as you can see, there are no returning passengers on the *Sealth*. Please do not be alarmed. As many of you know, an outbreak of some sort has occurred on one or more of the San Juan Islands. As a precaution, all island residents and visitors wishing to sail to the mainland have been put under observation for an unspecified amount of time. The Center for Disease Control has setup a water-bound quarantine site on the *Evergreen State* ferry and your loved ones are safe there. I am also told that quarantine reaches to all communications to unaffected civilians as well. This is only temporary and on behalf of the CDC and the Washington State Ferries, we thank you for your cooperation and understanding."

A sudden forward surge of the crowd summoned an army of police. They forced the scared civilians back to a safe distance. "Safe" meaning that they had plenty of time to apprehend someone who might attempt to board the private sailing.

Brett and the others in his group drove their vehicles on and slowly made their way up to the passenger area. The mad rush for window seats, a common occurrence on all ferries, never happened with the small group as they had the entire ferry to themselves.

Brett fed a coffee vending machine a handful of change collected from his pockets and watched its every motion. A cup fell haphazardly from out of nowhere to sit perfectly under the stream of hot coffee flowing out.

"Mr. McKay, can you take a seat, please?" a woman asked with a hint of impatience in her voice.

"I'm at the mercy of the coffee vending gods," Brett answered. When the machine had finally completed its cycle, he took his hot coffee and joined the others for a briefing.

"My name is Joanie, but you won't need to remember that. You all know your jobs. I don't want anyone taking unnecessary risks," the woman addressed the group. "Just take your notes, observe what you can and get back to the bed and breakfast before dark."

"Ooh, Bed and Breakfast? That sounds fancy," one of the others said.

"It isn't. It's an old farm, surrounded by men with guns and the woods around it are filled with infected islanders. Not exactly a dream vacation," Joanie said, effectively crushing anyone's visions of luxury on island time. "Do any of you have questions about what we've been seeing so far from the infected? Or about anything else?"

"This boat takes forever," a man sitting next to Brett complained. "Why couldn't we fly in?"

Joanie laughed. "Did you read the briefing? The airport is a hot zone. It's where the problem started. If we tried to fly in we'd be surrounded before the landing gear stopped rolling."

"Plus, a boat ride gives us more time for exciting meetings about information we already know," the woman on the other side of Brett joked.

Brett sipped his still hot coffee and spoke, "are any of you really in a hurry to get to Orcas? Things are a mess there. I'll take the boat as long as I can have it."

"I get sea sick," the woman beside him explained. "I *am* sea sick."

"Still," Brett said, "sea sick is better than infected with a mysterious disease. Does anyone know where the flight originated?" Brett asked, fearful of the answer.

"Good question," Joanie said, "Another island, Lopez, to the south."

"This is happening on Lopez as well?" another of the researchers asked.

"Everything in operation you see here, it's happening over there too. Teams of specialists, off-shore quarantine center, all of it."

"What, someone just sent a virus-laden plane island hopping?" the seasick woman asked, confused.

"That's what it looks like. A passenger was dropped at Lopez, and the pilot continued. The pilot was very ill when he crash landed."

"Let me guess, the dropped passenger was sick too?"

"Yep. And the islanders offered aid which only spread the disease."

After the meeting, Brett moved to one of the large windows on one side of the passenger deck. The snow had stopped but the sky was still overcast, making the tops of the islands disappear into the clouds. He closed his eyes and tried to imagine the trip across the water on a rare sunny day. The ferry engine's constant vibration and hum nearly lulled him to sleep, but his teammates kept throwing around wild stories around about cannibalistic humans running amok on Orcas.

The Sealth wound through the island chain with more purpose than usual. The water, a steely blue, was calmer between the dots of land. Diving birds stuck to business as usual, disappearing beneath the salt water for food and reappearing moments later in a new location on the water's surface. Approaching Orcas, the island looked beautiful and isolated. It was difficult to see any distress from the water. The highs cliffs a dead end and the low, pebbled beaches were only an option for escape if one owned a kayak. Brett could see a few kayakers bobbing in the waves. It was cold out and many of them had taken to the water in only their pajamas, shivering, blue-cheeked, and hungry. A small motorboat corralled them like lost sheep, toward the offshore quarantine site, an anchored ferry eerily dead in the water.

Everyone trying to leave the island was subject to quarantine protocol. The airport on the northern part of the island was shut down. No flights in or out. Any personal watercrafts leaving the island were subject to search.

The survey team disembarked at the ferry terminal. The relatively short line of vehicles was capped on either end by hired security. The stereotypical all-black Suburbans inspired, in most people, a feeling of safety, organization and control. As the line of cars snaked along the country roads toward Eastsound, the largest town on the island, Brett expected to see chaos but instead saw sprawling farms at the base of gentle peaks and a lot of cows.

"Looks ok here to me," Brett said to himself.

The convoy pulled down a long gravel road and up to a large two-story farmhouse-turned-bed and breakfast-turned base camp. The place had definitely lost some of its charm with the heavily armed men guarding the doors to its country-chic decorated rooms. Huge spotlights had been installed in the fields surrounding it. Brett felt relatively safe and his bed was firm, just the way he liked it. After everyone settled into their accommodations, they gathered in a sitting room to look over a map.

Kogan, one of the guards, explained the geography of the island, where the airport was (north), and the planned route for the next day.

"So, the affected area cut off the eastern side of the island?" one of the scientists on the team asked for clarification.

"Yes, but realistically, anyone stuck there is safe provided they stay indoors and are well-stocked on supplies. The trouble comes when people start wandering out for food or to investigate noises. That's when they get attacked and that's how the infection continues to spread," Joanie, the stern woman from the ferry, explained.

"And what's worse, in these types of situations, is that by the time people are forced out for sustenance, they are usually weakened from nutrient deficiencies. They are even less equipped to defend themselves."

"It's a perfect system," Mackenzie, one of the other researchers, said eerily.

"Not quite perfect," Berne countered. "The infection still needs full on contact and transmission of fluids for transfer. It isn't airborne. So as long as people can outrun the infected, they can escape infection."

I hate running, Brett thought.

Dinner was full of talk about 'directives' and 'shoot to kill orders'; the latter was hard to digest as he stared into the blood red borscht of the soup course. He tuned it out as he wasn't carrying a gun. He had his notebooks, a pain-in-the-ass laptop and a digital camera, as he was there to record, document, and analyze.

Joanie was seated at the head of the table. She rose at the end of dinner and addressed the group. "Please try to get some sleep tonight. You may hear gunshots. We've installed an alarm. If you don't hear the alarm, there's nothing to be *alarmed* about." She laughed at her choice of words. "Tomorrow will be a long day."

The next morning a knock came on the door of Brett's room. Upon opening it, he saw Kogan, who had been assigned his personal guard. Kogan eyed Brett up and down with a displeased look at his disheveled hair and attire, which consisted of a pair of boxers and a plain white tee.

"Get a move on, we're heading out to tour the airport and the town in a half hour," he barked.

"Sure thing," Brett yawned groggily, "Can you get me some coffee?"

"No, but you can get some yourself," Kogan smiled and walked down the hall toward reception.

Half an hour later the convoy drove the remaining distance to Eastsound. In just one short day it had been overrun, its small main roads filled with the infected. From a distance it looked like a street fair, but up close things were far from festive. As, the Suburbans rolled through the center of town disfigured people swarmed the car and bumped into it without fear of being run down. Brett checked to make sure that his door was locked.

"They won't try to open it," one of the guards laughed.

"Just in case, though," Brett shuddered at the thought of being pulled from the vehicle and attacked. A man threw himself at Brett's window, his face pressing against the glass in desperation. Blood and flesh smeared on the pane. "This is disgusting. Are you sure we can't catch it?"

"Yep. Unless you want to lick the window or pucker up," Kogan laughed.

A scratchy voice reported something on the CB radio. It was unintelligible to Brett but the driver of the vehicle understood the message and translated for the rest of the group in the SUV.

"We have word that roughly ten uninfected citizens are trapped in a bar just off the main road here," the driver said. "I'm guessing it's that one," he pointed to a bar surrounded by haphazardly parked vehicles.

"Is someone going to help them?" Brett queried.

"There's a team for that. They have more guns and…no scientists," Kogan said with hints of jealousy and sadness in his voice.

Brett turned to face him. "I'm not a scientist and I didn't ask for a babysitter, so don't think for one second that I wanted to be tied to your hip."

The Suburban took them north to the airport, the source of the trouble, and with its bloodstained runway it was a sight to behold. A crash-landed plane sat mid-runway and injured people wandered around everywhere inside the fence. They moved toward the noise of the Suburban's engine.

"Ok," Joanie's voice came over the CB radio, "as you can see, this is ground zero. We're going to drop the investigative teams here. Please, stay outside of the fence and watch your back.

Brett made his way up the west fence line; Kogan was at his heels and on high alert. Countless numbers of infected islanders slowly walked across the runway and toward the duo. Because of the fence, Brett wasn't worried about being attacked. That is until he heard crunching leaves in the woods to his left.

A nude woman broke through the trees. She was eerily pale and missing an ear and half of her scalp, as though someone had ripped her hair and flesh off the bone. Kogan took aim and dispatched of her with one shot to the head.

"Can you give me a minute or two to study one of them before killing them? I can't do my job when they're dead."

"I have established a safe perimeter of one-hundred yards. When an infected comes within that distance, I pull this trigger."

"One-hundred yards? I'll need binoculars to study anything from that far away!"

Kogan opened one of the seven hundred pockets of his military vest and pulled a compact pair of binoculars from it. "Here you go."

"Don't play with me," Brett said as he pushed the binoculars back at Kogan's chest, "I don't *want* to need them. Can we tighten the perimeter? Or maybe find a high point to perch and watch for a while? You could save on ammo."

"All right, we could do that. But it's on you to find a good spot."

Before Brett could find a suitable place to observe from, Kogan's rifle exploded again. Brett spun on his feet, expecting to see an infected falling to the ground but no one was there. A moment later a bald eagle fell to the grass, a bullet wound in its neck.

"What the hell are you doing? We aren't here to kill endangered species!" Brett grabbed at the collar of Kogan's jacket, shaking him and causing his helmet to shift on his head.

"I have orders to shoot down anything that flies and that includes avians. Some of the doctors suggested they could be carriers and technically, all flights are grounded." He laughed a stupid chuckle at his closing quip. "Besides, they were taken off the endangered list years ago."

"But that is a *bald eagle*," Brett pointed at the dead bird.

"It *was* a bald eagle. If we can't figure this disease out, we are going to be endangered like it used to be."

It was the smartest and most frightening thing Brett had heard since arriving on the island. He looked down at the huge bird and its beauty. Judging solely on its outward appearance and apart from the fresh wound, Brett determined the eagle to be healthy.

"I don't think the eagle was a carrier." He squatted and started to take the lens off of his camera.

"No," Kogan said as he laid a hand on the lens, "no pictures of downed wildlife. You are here to study the infection."

"But they think birds could carry it, it *is* part of my study. How is it that you know all of these rules and I don't?" Brett questioned with frustration in his voice.

"Extra briefing," Kogan said, opening another one of the many pockets of his outfit, "the mission guide says that photography is strictly forbidden except by those with scientific clearance *and* in those cases, photography is to be limited to human subjects only."

"Why don't I have a mission guide?" Brett demanded.

"You didn't come to breakfast. They handed them out," Kogan shrugged.

"You could have grabbed an extra one for me! Didn't you think it might be important for me to have a copy?"

"Breakfast is important too. More important than lazing about in your ugly boxer shorts."

"That's it!" Brett yelled, yanking the guide from his hands and throwing it on the ground. "Next chance I get, I'm trading you in for a more considerate armed guard!"

"Good luck! We aren't paid to be considerate," Kogan laughed as he picked up the eagle and threw its body into the underbrush of the forest.

Brett was able to climb on top of an abandoned delivery truck and watch the infected. He took basic notes about their behavior but there wasn't much to say. They appeared to be lost or without cognition, and were violent when aware of any uninfected presence. Brett had never seen anything like it.

After hours of observation, the black Suburbans came back to collect the group and return them to the safety of the farmhouse.

Covered in dirt from climbing around and feeling generally dirty from having been near the infected, Brett went straight to one of the shared bathrooms in the farmhouse. He took a thorough shower and was wrapping his towel around his waist when he heard a familiar voice call out from one of the toilet stalls.

"They're calling it the San Juan Strain," the disembodied voice said.

"Uuuugh," Brett moaned. "That name is ridiculous."

"You have to admit that it rolls off the tongue," the voice responded.

"It sounds like something out of a horror novel and it will only inspire over-exaggerated headlines. Who are you?"

A man emerged from one of the stalls and Brett recognized him immediately.

"How did you get over here?" Brett asked the reporter he'd met on the mainland.

"I stowed away," the reporter smiled.

"I'm not even sure how that is possible but, ok."

"Someone on your team left their van unlocked on the ferry. I climbed in and breathed shallowly for forty-five minutes."

"Well, you can't tag along with me. I have an armed guard who is watching everything I do." Brett took a smaller towel to his head to dry his hair. "Well, almost everything."

"Speaking of your friend, would you care to comment on the expensive collection of highly-trained, weapon-toting gentlemen littering the island?"

"You don't have clearance. And I don't do interviews in the john," Brett replied, "it echoes. Now sneak out of here however you snuck in."

Brett stepped outside to gather his thoughts before dinner. He made his way to the back corner of the wrap-around-porch. He sat on the cold wood and draped his journal across his lap. The fields behind the building were covered in a delicate layer of frost, something he appreciated as a natural alarm system. After ten minutes of solitude and studying of his notes, he felt a presence behind him. He jumped with the anticipation of defending himself against an infected individual.

"Hey, hey! It's only me!" that same familiar voice called out. The reporter sat down next to Brett and leaned in to read his journal.

Brett snapped it closed. "I thought you left," he said.

"No, I just hung out in the woods for a bit," the reporter said.

"Did you see many infected?" Brett was impressed that the man would trot around in a forest, alone, with the infection running rampant on the island.

The reporter looked down at his feet. "They're everywhere out in the woods. And they looked to be heading for the ferry dock. You've been watching them. Do you think they can smell us?"

"I'm not sure. But something is telling them to follow the uninfected."

The reporter pulled a small booklet from his back pocket and opened to a cat-eared page. "I happened upon a copy of this mission guide and I have to say, it is an interesting read," he said.

"Oh great, you even have a mission guide." Brett was beginning to feel less and less a part of the mission at all.

"I found it on the ground out front in the driveway. If you're so hurt about it I can lend it to you but I'll need it back for my story."

"No, I'm not going to borrow the mission guide for my own operation from a reporter who isn't even supposed to be here!"

"I could make a photocopy," the reporter offered.

Brett said nothing in response as he stood up and went back inside, leaving the reporter in the cold.

Later that night, Brett was awakened by the sound of the frost-covered field being crunched by dozens of feet. He was out of bed and in full winter clothes before the guard sounded the alarm. It emitted a pitiful yowling sound and was too loud, like the speakers at a movie theater. He ran down the hall to reception.

"They should turn the siren off now that everyone has been alerted," Brett yelled to the woman at the reception desk who couldn't hear over the wailing and the heavy gunfire that had started. He covered his ears to show her that it was loud. She opened a drawer and handed Brett a pair of earplugs and a sedative.

"You want me to go back to sleep? Are you kidding me?" He threw the packaged earplugs and pills at her and then looked outside through the front doors to the fields and the tree line beyond. The infected were spilling out between the trunks and occasionally one would fall from a well-placed bullet.

On his way back down the hall to his room, Brett bumped into Mackenzie in the hall. "Did you get your plugs and pills?" he asked, pointing to his ears.

"What?" Brett had heard him, but didn't understand how Mackenzie knew they were available at the front desk.

"We have to get out of here!" Brett informed him. "The siren is drawing them out of the woods!"

"The guards can protect us!" Mackenzie yelled back.

Brett shook his head and went back to his room to pack his bag. He buried his field journal near the bottom for safekeeping. Outside, Brett had no idea where they'd parked his vehicle but he didn't need to know because the reporter pulled up in a small pickup truck. The passenger side window was rolled down and the reporter leaned over the front seat to wave Brett in, knowing he wouldn't be able to hear any words if he spoke them.

Brett rolled the window up, fearing the outstretched arms of the sick. They sped down the road in the truck, away from the farm and the town. Infected swarmed from the woods. At a stop sign, a bloodied woman hit the truck's passenger window with so much force that the glass fell into the doorframe.

"Jesus Christ, this thing is getting in! Why'd you stop?" Brett screamed.

The reporter pulled a handgun out from under the seat, "cover your ears!" he yelled at Brett.

He did as he was told and covered his ears the best he could. The reporter fired a single shot into the head of the beast and all was right inside the vehicle again.

"My ears are still ringing," Brett shouted.

"But you're alive," the reporter smiled.

The truck pulled up to the ferry loading area. Vehicles sat backed up the road. The reporter parked the car and Brett ran to find a recognizable face. He found Joanie, the leader of his group but she didn't look happy to see him.

"You shouldn't be here. Can I have someone take you back to the farmhouse?" she asked as she looked down at the blood on his shirt.

"This is more than I can take! I have blood all over me! I was almost infected! I just want off this fucking island!" Brett screamed.

"No, I don't think you do, Brett," she said calmly. "Just after you arrived we got a call. Our quarantine procedures were inadequate. The infection has reached the mainland."

- THE MAINLAND -

Michelle Kilmer and Rebecca Hansen

PERVERSION

His confidence had grown after six successful attacks at other campgrounds up and down the West Coast the previous summer. Women always felt safer in the gated ones and would go alone to the showers. It was there that Raymond Hyde found them.

This day was no different for him in the full campground. It was one of the last weekends that anyone would be caught out in the elements of usually rainy western Washington. He had no trouble finding the bath and shower building near the center of the grounds. Raymond took quick glances all around to make sure no one was watching and then slipped through the door. He heard running water and followed the sound around a half wall on one side of the room.

There she was, alone and unaware of his presence. The woman was still clothed in a tank top and hiking pants and she stood under the running water of the public showerhead. *That's odd,* the man thought. Normally they'd be wearing nothing more than a bathing suit and sometimes he was lucky to find them nude. Her clothing made his goal harder to reach but he wasn't about to pass up this prize.

Raymond approached her from behind but just as he reached her, she fell to the floor. A smile grew on his face. *Maybe she's drunk,* he hoped. In his experience, it took an inebriated woman longer to realize that she was being taken advantage of. He turned off the water and got to work tearing off her clothes. She was very limp in his hands.

Once he had her naked, he busied himself with the attack. He had to be quick for the sake of not getting caught and he had to be rough in order to get off because he was so desensitized. Just before he finished, her eyes shot open and she sat up abruptly.

"Whoa, Whoa woman. I'm in charge of this show!" Raymond slapped her face and forced her back to the floor. He was used to fighters but there was something very different about her. The woman was not screaming and that was unusual. It thrilled the twisted man though, because he didn't have to use a hand to stifle cries for help. With an extra free hand, he had even more power over the victim. Besides, she was trying to bite him and he didn't want to put his hands anywhere near her teeth. *Other men are caught that way,* he remembered. The police could match bite marks to teeth. Keeping injury free meant getting away with the crime.

Raymond held her down at the shoulders. She threw her head from side to side, seemingly desperate to injure him. Another unusual thing about this woman was her extraordinary aggression. It never waned. Women under attack often eventually submit but she wriggled relentlessly underneath him.

Unattractive gargling noises came from deep within her throat and made him lose interest. He decided then to kill her, but after five minutes of increasing grip around her neck and no change in her behavior, he was confused and pissed off. She lay naked, soaking wet and struggling, and still emitting the horrible gargling noise.

"If I can't kill you, I sure as hell can shut you up!" he yelled, cupping one hand firmly over her gaping mouth as he had to so many others. No sooner had her sounds been quieted did he let out a roar of pain. Her teeth ripped a healthy chunk of skin from the center of his palm.

"You bitch!" he screamed, slamming the woman's head repeatedly into the cement floor until she stopped struggling.

Raymond jumped to his feet and ran to the paper towel dispenser. He wrapped his hand in a dozen sheets and took temporary shelter in one of the stalls. He couldn't leave the restroom until the bleeding was under control.

Sitting on the grimy toilet, the smell of dirt and excrement rising from beneath him, he nursed his damaged hand until the plague had run its course within his body, killing and reanimating him into a new man.

Michelle Kilmer and Rebecca Hansen

SOMETHING AS A FAMILY

Sylvie walked back to the campsite from the restroom with tears falling from her eyes.

"Sylvie, did you find the bathroom?" Laurie asked her eight- year-old daughter. Along with her husband Glen, the three of them were staying in their camper at a developed campground for a week, at Laurie's urging. They'd arrived that morning and had just finished setting up camp. Sylvie was young but old enough for her mother to trust her safety in the enclosed and heavily monitored environment.

"Mommy," she cried, "there's a man in the girl bathroom."

Laurie jumped to her feet, away from the campfire she'd started, and walked to meet her child. "Glen!" she yelled. She pulled her daughter toward her in a tight hug. "Did he hurt you?" she asked.

Glen exited the camper with an armful of cooking utensils. He casually walked up to his wife and daughter. "What's up? Did you find the potty, Sylvie?"

"Some creep was in the bathroom!" Laurie screamed at him as she tried to calm the girl by caressing her head.

Glen dropped all of the utensils but a long hot-dog roasting stick and then took off in a run. He headed in the direction that he thought the restroom was. *I'll kill him!* his mind raged.

Pulling Sylvie away from her, Laurie asked again "Did he hurt you?"

The girl nodded her head and held out her arm. Droplets of blood hit the pine-needle-covered ground. "He bit me."

Laurie felt elation for a moment. Her daughter had not been molested; she wouldn't be traumatized for the rest of her life. That moment ended as Sylvie collapsed, sending whirls of dust and dirt into the air around her.

"Glen!" she yelled again as she scooped their only child up off the ground, but her husband was too far away to hear her now.

Glen approached the restrooms. A smell of urine mixed with chlorine, from the campground's pool, hung in the air with the flies. The building looked empty. Normally there would be a quickly forming line at either entrance but they'd come in the off-season to avoid the crowds.

Before using the entrance marked 'Ladies', he looked around the campground. He didn't want anyone to see him and think he was the pervert. When he was satisfied that no one was watching, he breached the doorway and stepped into the slightly dimmer girl's bathroom. As his eyes adjusted to the light he noticed that the room was identical to the men's side of the building. Dead bugs clung to the ventilation grate, mirrors that you couldn't see yourself in hung on one wall and scraps of toilet paper stuck to the wet, cement floor. The only difference was the lack of urinals.

"Ahhhhhhh," a deep voice echoed out from one of the three stalls, bouncing off the walls and high ceiling. To Glen it sounded like a moan of pleasure.

He wasn't comfortable with confrontation but Glen felt bold due to the circumstances and the fact that a metal stall door hung between him and the perpetrator. "You know, guys like you get killed in prison!" he blurted out before he lost the courage.

The man in the stall moaned louder which sickened Glen. *Maybe the guy gets off on trouble?* He thought. "Disgusting," Glen said as he pushed open the stall door. "Oh my God," he gasped when he saw what really stood behind it.

Laurie held her lifeless child as she ran as fast as she could to find her husband. The plain, dark brown building that was the restroom finally appeared through a stand of trees. When she reached the clearing in front of the building she felt her daughter stir in her arms.

"Oh, thank you Lord!" she exclaimed as, simultaneously, her husband exited the ladies restroom. "Glen, I think she fainted but she's ok now! Glen? Glen, are you ok?" Laurie watched her husband stumble and then fall to the ground just as Sylvie had done before.

"La- La- Laurie," Glen stammered, "he bit me." Laurie set Sylvie's small body on the ground next to him and looked his body over for the wound she knew she would find. Blood ran from a mouth-sized hole in his shoulder. She applied pressure to it, like she'd seen so many times on television but his conditioned worsened. "It wasn't a man," Glen said before breathing his last.

"I should have listened to you, Glen. We could have stayed home, but I just wanted to do something as a family." Laurie broke down over the body of her husband and cried for some time. When she finally forced herself to pull away she turned to see her daughter sitting up and someone slowly walking out of the restroom. It was a man but he looked unwell with no color in his skin and bloody paper towels stuck to one of his arms. Glen's hotdog roasting pole was sticking out from the man's chest.

Laurie screamed as Sylvie embraced her in a strange hug that stemmed more from hate than love. She was only silenced when her child's tiny mouth tore through her skin.

Before Laurie died, she watched her husband rise again.

PUBLIC HEALTH

"You need to go home, El," Ella's manager said to her.

"I'm going to finish my shift and then I'll go. I promise I'll stay home tomorrow if I still feel bad," she replied. Ella stood at a tiny backroom sink, rinsing blood off of her hand and down the drain before lightly re-bandaging it.

"I can't believe you! A car almost hits you, then you get cut trying to help the guy who was most likely dead and you *might* stay home tomorrow? Jeez," her manager sighed.

"The cut isn't bad. I'm a little shaken up but I really am OK to work," Ella said as convincingly as she could. She needed the money and couldn't take another day off if rent was going to be paid.

"At least it wasn't your dipping hand!" the manager joked. "But be sure to wear gloves."

"Yeah, ok," she said. She hated wearing the gloves. They made her hands sweat, especially in the heat of the small shop.

Ella was the ice cream girl in the Cone Shack, charged with making and serving the ten different flavors of dipped cones they sold. It wasn't a dream job but she could people watch out the service window when no one was in line.

She went to the storage closet to locate the box of latex gloves and smiled when she found the box was empty. "We're fresh out of gloves!" she yelled to her manager, who had stepped outside behind the building for a smoke.

"I was going on a supplies run anyway. I'll get some more. Don't serve any ice cream until I get back with them."

The manager left, leaving Ella to battle with the demanding young children that always approached with their mothers. She could see one of them coming from further down the strip mall.

Ella's body started to feel different at the same time one of the children dropped a handful of change on the service window's small ledge.

"Chocolate-dipped Chocolate!" the boy ordered.

"You're gonna have to wait. I can't serve the ice cream yet," Ella said through the fever she felt building inside of her.

"The sign, it says 'open' and my mom said I could have some," the boy reasoned.

A woman, whom Ella could only assume was the boy's mother, walked up to the window. Sirens roared by in the distance, causing everyone in the shopping center to crane their necks in the direction of the noise.

Ella felt faint and sweaty. Maybe I should have gone home, she thought. I must be in shock or something.

"Did you order your cone, hon?" the woman asked the boy at the window.

The boy nodded and Ella explained, "I can't . . . I can't serve it yet, ma'am. We're out of gloves." She could barely get the words out and she was feeling worse by the second.

The woman laughed at her. "I don't care about gloves! Here's the money, just give him the ice cream. We're in a hurry to get home. It's his birthday and we'll be late for the party!" The woman pulled a five-dollar bill from her wallet and stuck it in the tip jar to further convince Ella.

Ella knew she could lose her job if she disobeyed her manager's instructions but she felt so ill that it no longer mattered to her. All she wanted to do was serve the kid his chocolate-dipped chocolate and go lie down on the floor of the supply room. "Fine," she said and swiveled around on the stool that sat between the cash register and the ice cream machine.

Ella's injured hand had been hanging at her side, the blood dripping slowly to the floor. She lifted it to the ice cream lever and put a cone under the spout with the other hand. Blood still dripped to the floor but her body blocked the customers from seeing this grisly event. When the ice cream was done spiraling she pulled it away from the machine, through her dripping blood and directly into the chocolate shell dip.

"Here you go. Happy Birthday," she said to the boy.

CHECKED OUT

Marley drove his four-wheeler around the campground on regular patrol, usually every two hours or after someone new checked in. He had just returned from a round and the morning was off to a normal start until a teenager ran into the office muttering something about "a weirdo" by the bathroom.

"I'm on it," Marley said. He pushed the teen out of his office, grabbed a shovel and took his quad straight to the public bathrooms. In the past, drunken partiers would end up nude and rowdy at the showers, scaring the sober campers and their children. He had seen it all and was ready for anything.

Except for a man covered in blood and dirt.

Marley recognized the gentleman as Glen, a father and husband who had checked in earlier that morning. "Glen," he said, "you might want to have someone take a look at that wound."

Glen lunged at Marley, who was still on the ATV. He accelerated and moved a distance away but Glen continued to follow him.

"If something in the campground did that to you, I'd like to know. Your safety is important to me."

Glen reached again with dirty hands.

Marley once again drove forward a ways. "If you come closer I *will* smack you! I don't like feeling threatened, especially at my own campground!"

Again, Glen advanced.

"This is your last warning, Glen. I've got a mean swing."

Marley's intimidations did nothing to dissuade the man. He parked the four-wheeler and stood at the water's edge. Seeing that Glen was nearly upon him, Marley brought the shovel to his side and swung it forward like a bat. The force was so strong that Glen was knocked from his feet and dead on the spot. His body fell in the lake and slowly floated away with the current.

"Oh my, what have I done?" Marley said. He called over his walkie-talkie to his assistant back at the office. "Jerry, call the sheriff. There's a body in the lake."

The speaker crackled and Jerry's voice came calling back. "Did you say a body?"

"Don't ask questions, just call the sheriff and tell him to bring a boat around to the back access point. Tell him I don't want him bringing it through the campground. It could frighten campers."

As Marley drove slowly back through the wooded area he could see that many more campers were wounded and they all seemed to take a special interest in him. He killed the engine on the four-wheeler and walked briskly to the center of the grounds. As he moved, the campers followed him more fervently and their numbers grew until it seemed as though the entire roster of families was accounted for in the mass.

He flung the shovel behind him desperately as the horde of maniacal campers chased him through the campground. He snaked through the rows of RVs trying to shake them. When he saw the lights on in an Airstream, he approached with caution. The curtains were drawn so he couldn't tell what might be inside.

He risked knocking on the door and he could hear scared whispering on the other side. Words like "mom" and "them" were thrown around; a small child was crying. Marley knocked again with more urgency but a man inside told him to "go away!"

Behind him, feet dragged through the gravel on the roadway, signaling to him that the crazed people had caught up. He had to choose between making a run to his office, through their path, or hiding in one of the many tents until they moved on.

He spotted a four-person model with its rainfly on that would hide him well. "Hello," he whispered, scratching on the tent in an attempt to knock. "Is anyone in there?" When no one answered, Marley threw the zipper open and jumped inside.

The group shambled past, like so many buffalo migrating; bursts of angry activity rippled through them. When he thought they were gone, he started to unzip the tent but his walkie-talkie rang out a desperate call.

"Marley! I'm trapped inside the tool shed," his maintenance worker called out, "Some nut—"

Marley lay on the speaker to diminish its noise. His hand finally found the switch to turn it off but not before the sound drew the crowd of infected back. Shadows grew on the nylon walls and Marley let out a small yelp. The plagued people descended with a snapping and tearing of tent, flesh and bone.

RECIPE FOR DISASTER

Marilyn pulled up to the tri-level they called their home. She looked at her son in the rear-view mirror. His sun-tanned face and part of his chest were smeared a darker brown from the chocolate-dipped chocolate ice cream cone he'd devoured.

"Uugh, Brandon! Your party starts in twenty minutes. I'll have to run you a bath."

"I don't feel good," Brandon whined, holding his belly.

"Chocolate-dipped stomachache. You shouldn't have downed it so fast, kiddo," Marilyn said as she put the car in park and killed the engine. "Now, up to the bathroom! Your friends will be here any minute!"

"Presents!" Brandon exclaimed as he skipped, chocolate-covered and still clutching his belly, through the front door.

Marilyn finished filling the tub for her son and went downstairs to finish decorating for the party. After the streamers were up and the cake was laid out she got to work mixing the punch.

At three o'clock Brandon's friends and their parents, mostly mothers, started to arrive. Diane, a neighbor and mother of Brandon's closest friend Nathaniel, stopped Marilyn in the entrance to the house. "Laurie wanted me to let you know they couldn't make it. She and Glen took Sylvie camping at one of those luxury campgrounds."

"Sounds fancy! I'm sure they're having loads of fun. It's nice to see *you* though!" Marilyn said.

She then addressed the other guests, who were more acquaintances than friends. "The party will be outside, on the back patio," Marilyn pointed to the backyard, "gifts can go beside the food table."

What is Brandon up to? Marilyn wondered. She climbed the first flight of stairs to look for him. "Brandon?" she called down the hall. "Honey, your friends are all here now." He didn't respond and after a thorough search, she went back downstairs to try her luck there.

Approaching the kitchen, she heard a *slurping* sound. "Brandon?" she called out again as she turned the corner to the kitchen. "Caught you red handed!" Marilyn played. Brandon was sitting on the counter top drinking straight from the punch bowl.

"What are you doing?" she asked.

"Trying to help my tummy," he said weakly. He had dressed himself after his bath but he'd barely dried his hair and it now dripped onto his shirt, leaving darker wet patches across his shoulders.

Marilyn felt her son's face. He didn't feel hot but his forehead was sweaty. "Stay here, let me get a towel." Marilyn went to the linen closet for something to dry him off.

Brandon leaned forward, staring at his reflection in the punch. A string of drool involuntarily left his lip and fell into the bowl, the pink fluid absorbing it as though it had never fallen in.

"Oops," Brandon said as he climbed off the counter.

His mother returned and gave him a quick rub down to make him as presentable as possible. "Let's just get through the party, ok?" she asked as she carried the punch bowl to the back patio.

"There he is!" one of the mothers exclaimed.

"Happy Birthday, Brandon!" the children in attendance said in unison.

Marilyn set the punch down and gave it a quick stir with the ladle to remix the ingredients. "Feel free to grab a drink everyone!"

"Oh, is this the famous punch recipe I've been hearing about?" Diane asked.

"Sure is. I don't think it will make the news or anything, but it's pretty good," Marilyn said humbly.

Diane took a sip of the full cup she was offered. "Are you kidding me? Marilyn, this is amazing! Don and I are having a little party this weekend. You have to give me the recipe!"

"'I'd like to try some too!" Another mother took a cup and Marilyn filled the remaining ones.

Brandon set to opening his presents while his friends and their moms nibbled on the snacks his mom had made. When he had finished, the punch bowl was empty and he could no longer feel his hands.

"Mom, my hands," Brandon said, holding them up limply.

She rubbed them but it did little to restore feeling. "Ok, maybe you should go lay down. I'll bring your presents in and say goodbye to your friends for you."

Brandon staggered into the house. He made it to the foot of the stairs before his legs stopped working.

She walked to a central part of the backyard and yelled over the children playing. "Everyone, thank you *so* much for coming! Brandon is feeling unwell, maybe from all of the sugar he's had today, so we're calling it a day. Please take some cake home with you!"

Diane was the last guest to leave. "Thanks for the invite, Nathaniel had a great time," she said. "You know, I live down the street. One of these days I'm going to find out what you put in that punch!"

JUST A LITTLE SNAG

Don's bait jar was empty. He'd been out at the lake all day, casting and losing bait to the weeds. He'd had a small amount of success; three fish floated on the water, tethered to the dock on a hard plastic rope he slipped through their gills. It wasn't his best haul but it was enough for him, his wife and their son.

He looked across the lake and a mile beyond, where he knew the freeway lie. He looked at his watch.

"Shit. Traffic's going to suck." Driving at this time would add thirty minutes or more to his trip. Don decided to keep casting his empty line to waste time. There was a risk that the sharp hook would catch on the thick weeds or garbage that littered the bottom of the lake.

"Just keep the line moving," he told himself.

Some time after his tenth cast the hook snagged on something and wouldn't come loose. Don refused to cut the line and lose his sinking weight and hook to the lake. His wife Diane had told him there wasn't room in the family budget for more fishing paraphernalia, for a while anyway. He'd have to try harder to save it.

Don tugged on the line, sending his fishing pole high into the air and arcing with tension. He paced back and forth on the dock, trying different angles. Sometimes this helped to free the snag, if one was lucky. He let some slack out on the line, allowed it to rest and then reeled it back in for all he was worth. To his surprise, the hook broke free of its ensnarement and came happily back with the rest of the line.

"What is that?" Don said, looking at a clump of material that still clung to the hook. The weeds in the lake were a vibrant green, not a grayish-black like this was. He set his pole against the dock's railing to grab the line and examine the hook more closely.

Whoop. A police boat wailed causing Don to jump and the dirty hook to impale one of his fingers.

"Damn it!" he yelled, withdrawing the hook. He clasped it onto one of the pole's line guides and scanned the lake for the police. A boat slowly approached the dock; men on board scanned the water while a diver suited up.

"Sir," a man on a megaphone said in Don's direction, "you can't fish anymore. The lake is closed."

"Closed?" Don yelled. "I've never heard of a lake closing during fishing season!"

"It's closed, sir, and I can't give you more information than that. Please pack your things and get home."

"Ok," Don said quietly. With gear in hand he took the dock back to the shore and his vehicle, occasionally looking back to the water. *Looks like a missing persons search to me*, Don speculated.

Ten minutes later he'd made it to the freeway but he'd only succeeded in merging into the mess. His car sat idling, his pricked finger ached and the backup of vehicles was much worse than usual. He scanned the radio for information, finding a lot of strange stories but nothing related to the traffic jam.

"Diane is going to be pissed," Don said aloud. He'd been late for dinner several times that week already. His son Nathaniel would be more forgiving, especially when he saw the fresh fish that lay in the ice chest in the back of his dad's Jeep.

Don could see people getting out of their vehicles ahead of him to get a better look at what was causing the delay. He turned off the engine of his car, which set off a chain-reaction of horn honks from drivers behind him, and grabbed his jacket.

Once outside of his warm Jeep he was glad he had his coat. The sun was down and the air had an uncomfortable bite to it. In the pocket of his jacket his cell phone rang. "Hello?" he asked without checking the screen.

"Don, wh- where are you?" a raspy voiced asked on the other end. Don barely recognized it as belonging to his wife.

"I'm so sorry. I know I'm late again. It's the traffic this time, I swear it," he told her.

"Something's wrong. We're sick." Diane's teeth chattered after the words left her mouth. It was so loud that Don could hear it through the phone.

"You lay down until I get home. I'll be there soon," Don replied comfortingly.

"Y- y- you don't underst-" Diane's voice faded as though she'd dropped the phone.

"Diane? Honey? Diane!" Don yelled. Other motorists turned at the spectacle he was making. He shoved his phone back into his pocket and took off running down the middle of the bumper-to-bumper freeway toward the next exit.

He quickly started to sweat, so profusely that he had to remove his jacket. As his heart beat faster from the exertion he began to lose feeling in his toes and fingertips. His jacket dropped from his loosening grip and his legs slowed until he was no longer running but staggering and clipping side mirrors with his numbing arms.

Don wasn't sure what was happening to him but it seemed that he'd caught more than fish that day.

NO ESCAPE

Within sight of their exit, traffic had come to a standstill. On any other day this hold up would not have bothered Lia, but Jack's stubbornness had hit an all-time high and she couldn't escape it.

"I don't understand why you couldn't have just pretended to be interested in being there," Lia said. "My parents were really looking forward to meeting you."

With the sound of horns coming from behind, Jack's attention turned from Lia as he peered out of his driver side mirror to see what was going on. "What the fuck is this guy doing?" Jack mumbled.

"Are you even listening to me? Have you heard anything I've said?" Lia's voice grew louder as she tried to regain Jack's attention.

Jack turned toward Lia. "Your DAD was on his fucking cell phone half the time while your mom kept checking the clock!"

"My dad was on the phone trying to reach his auto mechanic to fix this piece of crap Volvo," Lia explained as she hit the dashboard, "and my mom was baking cookies for us! They were only trying to help!"

"We don't need their help" Jack whispered as he caught glimpse of something out of the corner of his eye. "We don't need anyone's help!"

Thunk.

"Seriously?" Jack said as a man in a fishing vest, full of various lures and hooks, fell against the left side of the Volvo, scraping the paint as he slid to the ground.

Jack reached for the door handle but Lia stopped him from opening it. "Stay inside," she said. "We don't know what's wrong with him."

"I don't care what's wrong with him. He's paying for a new paint job," Jack decided as he opened the door.

He found the man resting against the rear tire, hunched forward and sluggishly trying to stand up again. The man's wallet lay open on the asphalt between them.

"I'm just going to get your insurance information." Jack reached for the wallet as he mumbled, "Fucking drunk". Suddenly the man lunged forward, moving much faster than he had before; teeth sunk into Jack's arm and broke skin as Jack pulled away.

"Shit man, how much more damage are you gonna cause?" Jack took the small amount of cash that was in the wallet and threw it back at the man. Around him, other motorists began locking their doors hoping to distance themselves from the violent man and the thief who were making a scene.

Jack climbed back into the car and was immediately berated by Lia, "First you piss off my parents, then you ignore me and now you've just robbed a drunk man?"

"I've heard of angry drunks, but this is something else," Jack said as he surveyed the damage to his forearm. "I am sick of this traffic jam, we're taking the shoulder."

"I'd tell you not to but I know you wouldn't listen," Lia said, resigned.

With a hard right turn of the wheel, Jack slowly accelerated, leaving the chaos behind them. He made it to the off ramp and without looking merged onto the road that would take them back to their apartment.

A few blocks from home Lia grew concerned as her boyfriend grew pale and sweaty. She placed a hand to his forehead but he immediately brushed it away.

"You don't look so hot, Jack. Maybe we should stop by the walk-in clinic?"

"I just want to be at home, in my bed," he said angrily.

The remainder of the drive and walk to the apartment from the car were silent. In the hallway, Jack was losing his balance as Lia fought to support his failing body.

"What's wrong with him?" asked Amber, the girl from across the hall. "He looks like shit!"

Jack slowly lifted his head and spit in her face. "Piece of trash."

"Jack!" Lia yelled. "I'm sorry, Amber, he's had a rough day."

"Ugh, it got in my eye," Amber complained as she rubbed her face. "Did it ruin my makeup?"

"Yeah, you might want to touch it up a little, sorry," Lia said as she maneuvered Jack into their apartment.

Jack felt himself getting weaker by the second. He turned to Lia and said, "Maybe we do need someone's help."

SPECIALLY TRANSMITTED DISEASE

Amber heard the knock on her door that she'd been waiting for. "Coming!" she yelled as she finished tying her hair up. She gave herself one more look in the hallway mirror before answering the door. "You look good," she told herself.

"Hey," Trent said to her, inviting himself into her apartment, "you look nice."

"Thanks. I had to re-do my makeup after the guy down the hall fucked it up."

Trent wasn't protective of Amber, she was only a booty call, but he didn't want any other guy touching her like he did. "What did he do to you?" he asked her with a hint of accusation.

"Gross, it wasn't like *that*. He has a girlfriend and he's slightly less attractive than you. Don't worry," she told him. "He just spit in my face."

"What did you do to deserve that?" he asked. Trent knew that she could be difficult. He went into her kitchen and started looking through the refrigerator. Amber followed him.

"I might have said he looked like shit," she admitted. "He was stumbling all over the place. His poor girlfriend was practically dragging him into their apartment. Don't drink all my milk!" She smacked Trent's shoulder and took the half empty jug from his hands.

"No one likes to be told they look like shit," Trent said.

Amber was growing impatient and tired of talking. She ran her hands down Trent's chest and pulled him toward her bedroom. "Well, you sir, can say whatever you want." He willingly undressed and got to work doing what he was there for. Ten minutes into their make out session, Amber pushed him away.

"Ugh, my mouth is super dry and I'm all sweaty. It's weird," she told him.

"It's not weird to be sweaty right now. I'm sweaty too."

"Can you just get me some water? I feel horrible," Amber moaned.

"Yeah, sure," Trent said. He pushed himself up from the bed and started toward the bathroom. As he walked by his pants, his cellphone rang.

"Ignore it," Amber directed.

"It might be work," Trent shot back, grabbing the phone from a back pocket of his jeans. He carried the phone into the bathroom before answering because he could see from the screen that it was his girlfriend, Brenna. He closed the door and took the call.

"Hey, babe," Trent said as calmly as possible.

"Is that all? Just 'hey babe'? Did you forget?" Brenna yelled. She seemed pissed off already but he didn't know why.

Trent was confused. "Hmm?" he wanted it to sound more like he hadn't heard the question than that his answer would be the one she didn't want to hear.

"You did, didn't you? Our one year anniversary is today, Trent." Brenna was becoming more agitated by the second.

"I didn't forget! I'm out buying flowers," Trent lied. "I'll be home soon."

"Come back to bed!" Amber whined from the bedroom. Luckily for Trent the walls and doors were thick in the apartment and they muffled her words just enough.

"Who is that?" Brenna asked. "Are you with someone?"

"That was the flower lady. She asked if you like white or red." Trent's heart was racing and his sweaty palm was about to lose its grip on his cellphone.

"Oh," Brenna said, "tell her I like red."

"Ok, I will babe. I have to go pay now. I'll see you in a bit."

"I love you!" she said.

"You too," Trent said, avoiding the exact words she'd spoken to him. He hung up the call and turned to the sink to get a cup of water. When he got back to the bed, Amber's condition had deteriorated.

"Hey, here's the water," he said to her.

Amber weakly held up an arm but the cup dropped to the floor when her fingers failed to grasp it, water spilling on Trent's jeans. "I'm so – sorry," she stammered.

"I think you might be sick, Amber. And that was work on the phone, so I'm leaving for now," Trent said as he pulled on his wet jeans. "Text me when you feel better."

"Please st-st-stay," she said.

"I really have to go. Eat some soup or something." Trent backed out of the bedroom. He was worried that she was contagious. He'd already missed too much work as it was, juggling two relationships. He showed himself out of her apartment. In an apartment across the hall, Trent heard a woman screaming. He figured it was a fight caused by the dude who'd spit on Amber.

Twenty minutes later he made it home, stopping by a mini-mart to grab some flowers. Just moments after setting down his house keys, Brenna jumped on him in a large bear hug.

"Hi to you too," Trent said, kissing her forehead lightly.

Brenna stepped back, allowing him room to remove his jacket. "Your pants are soaked. What happened?"

Trent had forgotten to come up with an answer to that question. Thinking fast he said, "the flowers leaked on me." He handed her the bouquet, which he hoped she wouldn't notice was dry.

Brenna accepted the flowers but scrutinized them just as she had his pants. "I told you that I like red. These are white."

"They were all out of red, babe. It's what she gave me," Trent lied, digging his grave slightly deeper.

"Why would she give you a choice if all they had was white?" Brenna's voice was heavy with suspicion.

"She had some red roses but they were already wilted. I picked the white ones because they were still pretty, like you." Trent smiled as large as he could but his mouth was feeling dry, causing it to hurt.

"So they did have red," Brenna said. "Why are you lying to me?"

"I'm not babe, I'm just tired. Work was tough and people are acting strange all over town. I want to relax."

Brenna couldn't stay angry with him long. She put the flowers in water, grabbed Trent a beer and led him to the bedroom.

Trent was feeling déjà vu, which happened to him a lot since he technically lived two lives. "I'm not feeling up to anything right now. I think I'm coming down with something."

"Trent, don't pull this. It's our anniversary and I want you to make me feel special. And, I got something from the *toy* store today." Brenna pulled handcuffs from a gift bag. She climbed onto the bed and cuffed a wrist to the bedpost.

"This isn't like you, Brenna. Are you sure *you're* feeling ok?" Trent asked incredulously.

"Just cuff my other wrist and show me how much you love me!" Brenna yelled, shoving her non-cuffed wrist in his face.

Trent did as he was told. Once Brenna was cuffed tightly he started to kiss her neck, which she hated because it tickled her. Brenna smelled something floral on his skin, a scent much stronger than that of the flowers. "You smell like a girl," she told him.

"Can't be, I'm all man," Trent joked nervously and continued kissing her but lower so Brenna would lose the scent.

"No, Trent, stop! I'm serious! You slept with someone else!" Brenna's suspicion earlier had grown into confidence. "Who was it? Tell me!"

As if to confirm his infidelity his cellphone rang from the nightstand. The screen glowed in the darkened room and the name 'Amber' was clearly visible to Brenna. Trent reached for the phone and stood up to leave the room but his body swayed on weakened legs.

"Don't you answer that! Don't you fucking answer that call! Takes these cuffs off Trent!" Brenna screamed at her boyfriend. Trent turned to face her, answered the phone call and then collapsed at the foot of the bed, out of her sight. The phone dropped to the floor but Brenna could hear wheezing coming through the receiver.

"Oh my god, Trent? Are you ok?" she asked, unable to move from her position at the head of the bed. "Trent?" The wheezing on the phone turned to rag-filled screams.

No sound came from Trent's direction. Brenna's emotions skipped from anger and hurt to worry in a second. She looked to the cuffs to see if she could escape her restraints but they were too tight and the key was unreachable in the gift bag on the floor.

"Trent, answer me! What's wrong with you?" Brenna screamed. A grunt came from the floor and then she saw movement. A shoulder appeared and the rest of Trent's body followed. Brenna struggled against the cuffs causing the metal to hit the wood of the bedposts. Trent turned toward the noise and emitted sound once more in the form of a carnal growl.

"What the FUCK is wrong with you?" Brenna yelled. "Let me fucking go!"

Trent clambered onto the bed and toward his girlfriend. Brenna tucked her legs close to her body, screaming the entire time and working her way as close to the headboard as possible but Trent was relentless in his pursuit of what he wanted.

Brenna felt his breath on her neck and she smelled that sickly, flowery perfume on his skin. "What the hell did that bitch give you?" she screamed as he bit into her flesh.

Michelle Kilmer and Rebecca Hansen

RAMPAGE

Back at Jack and Lia's apartment things had turned from bad to worse. Jack lay face up in the hallway outside the bathroom. Lia had attempted to get him to the toilet thinking he was sick with the flu and might have to vomit. They'd only made it that far when Jack's body went limp. Lia struggled to hold him up but couldn't and he fell back to the floor. His heart was racing and he was sweaty but his body was cold. He was confused and tried to speak but Lia couldn't make out what he was saying. Panicking, she called 911 but no one answered.

"Come on, come on," Lia said softly hoping someone would pick up. "Why isn't anyone answering? It's *911*, someone has got to answer!"

A choking sound came from Jacks throat, then a long deep exhale.

"Jack, JACK! Breathe, Jack. Please breathe for me." Lia gave him a few quick smacks on the cheek. "Shit, Shit, Shit," she hissed. "What the fuck do I do, Jack?" she asked, half expecting a response. "Why do you have to be so confrontational?"

Lia stood up, entered the bathroom and hastily wet a washcloth. She was so caught up in being mad that she hadn't realized he'd taken his last breath and risen again. He appeared behind her in the mirror, pale and with an angry look on his face.

"Are you...OK?" she asked, the fear resonating in her voice. A second passed before he lunged at her, snarling like a rabid dog.

"JACK!" she yelled as she ducked right and through another door that led from the bathroom to their bedroom. She slammed the door quickly keeping Jack on the other side.

"What is WRONG with you? First you spit on Amber in the hall and now you're acting like some crazy nut job!"

Errrgghh

"Why are you making such weird noises, Jack? Just talk to me." Lia was more confused than worried now as she leaned up against the door that separated them. "Jack?"

BANG BANG BANG

He pounded on the door, the thin wood flexing with each blow.

"Please stop, Jack. You're *scaring* me," Lia started crying, the sound pulling Jack further through the door. She could hear the wood breaking. Suddenly realizing she was in danger she ran to the closet. "Where is it?" she whispered. Jack's dad had given him a gun for Christmas a few years prior and Lia was not happy about it, especially given Jacks tendency to overreact to the smallest of situations. She was slightly comforted though when he'd agreed to store it in the closet and to not take it out unless there was an emergency.

"This qualifies as a fucking emergency!" she said as she hurriedly opened the metal box and lifted the gun from it. "Never thought I'd be happy to see you."

Lia turned just in time to see the light from the bathroom coming through a small opening Jack had created in the door, his hand reaching through and pulling viciously at the wood. The rage with which he had attacked the door had caused large cuts on his hands but it didn't seem to matter. Blood caked them and the wood surrounding the hole. Like a scene from The Shining, Jack stuck his head through the opening as he pulled further at the damaged door.

"I'll shoot you if I have to Jack!" Lia yelled. She was braced against the bedroom wall near a bedside table, her arms elongated with the gun in a tight grip and pointed in the direction of the bathroom. The cavity in the door was large enough now that Jacks entire upper body was leaning through it and reaching for her. The movement of his flailing arms sent him falling through and to the floor. He got back up on his feet quickly and ran toward her.

"Don't make me do this!" Lia yelled as she pulled the trigger.

Jack's neck bent backwards as the bullet ripped through his skull and out the back of his head, sending blood and brains flying across the room. His lifeless body collapsed.

"I told you I'd shoot you," Lia said as she jumped over Jack's body, grabbed her keys from the living room and ran to the first place she could think to go. Amber's door was slightly ajar and the apartment was dim. Hoping she had calmed down from the earlier run in with Jack, Lia opened the door and entered the apartment. Amber was nowhere in sight.

Lia heard a soft noise coming from another room as she turned on the light in the entryway.

"Amber?" she said quietly as she walked through the kitchen and into a room that looked like a home office. In the corner, facing the wall was Amber.

"Hey, can we talk?"

Amber's head cocked sideways as if to acknowledge the question. Her body was crooked as she turned to face Lia. The same anger that had erupted in Jack had also overcome Amber as she displayed her teeth. Lia wasted no time in shooting her, this time though it was with a shot to her shoulder. Amber snapped back and moved toward Lia. A follow-up shot to the head stopped her dead in her tracks.

She spent no time thinking about what had just happened and instead turned around and left the apartment. Lia walked a short distance down the hall before she came across and man and a woman both running frantically toward her. Her heart started racing as she raised the gun and shot the man in the forehead.

"NO!" the woman yelled as she crouched behind a trash bin just under the mailboxes. "Why did you shoot him? He wasn't sick!"

Lia looked behind the woman and noticed a group of people gathered outside the main door to the building, they looked crazed and were forcibly trying to break through the glass.

"What's wrong with everyone?"

"They're infected, that's what we were running away from when you shot Dan. We were running away from THEM!" the woman said furiously.

Lia dropped her keys and said faintly, "I thought he was going to hurt me, just like Jack and Amber." A great sadness came over her, had she mistakenly killed her boyfriend and her neighbor as well? Or were they also 'infected'?

Doubt and the fact that she would never know the answer overwhelmed her.

"I killed Jack," Lia said abruptly as she pointed the barrel of the gun to the underside of her chin and pulled the trigger.

Michelle Kilmer and Rebecca Hansen

DON'T SWEAT IT

The yoga class was slowly filling, but only half of the usual number of students arrived by the designated start time. The instructor, a young woman named Brenna, was late and unreachable by phone, even after several attempts. Her manager, Mara was frustrated to the point of storming around the office.

"It's fine, Mara," Winnie, a fellow yoga instructor, said, "She's probably fighting with her boyfriend again. Trent's such a jerk."

"It's not fine at all! We have people waiting for her! People who showed up even though there's crazy stuff going on!" Mara yelled.

"Don't worry about it. She's just tied up or something. I'll sub. No one showed up for my morning class," Winnie offered.

"Ok, but this is the last time I'm allowing you to cover for Brenna," Mara stressed. "She's dead!" she hissed as she picked up the office phone and tried reaching the tardy teacher once more.

The wood-floored room was a balmy 90 degrees and gentle music played from overhead speakers. Twelve bare-footed and serious-looking yoga students, with their mats laid equally spaced four per row, sat cross-legged and ready to stretch and sweat. In the back row Raina was already feeling the heat. She had taken her daughter to a birthday party earlier but the festivities hadn't lasted very long because the boy felt sick. *Was he contagious?* She wondered as she felt a chill go through her body. Thankfully, the postures started out easy, with a few seated positions and then on to standing poses.

"Next we'll stand for Eagle Pose or 'Garurasana'," the teacher instructed.

Raina struggled to stand. Once on her feet, she raised one leg and tucked the foot into the inside of her other leg. It was then that she lost the feeling in her toes and feet. She broke from the pose and shook her feet to regain blood flow but it didn't help. She waited for the class to move to the next posture, hoping that the feeling in her lower limbs would return.

"And from here we'll move into 'Utkatasana' better known as Chair Pose." The instructor inhaled and brought her arms above her head and then bent her knees until they were nearly parallel to the floor.

Raina could barely lift her now numbing arms and she had the horrible sensation that her legs were no longer able to support her. She risked bending her knees as the teacher had shown but before she could reach the desired parallel position, her legs collapsed under her and she fell to her mat. She lay on the floor in what looked like Corpse Pose.

"Are you all right, ma'am?" Winnie called to the back of the room.

"I...I can't feel anything. I can't move," Raina uttered. Her voice, though quiet, echoed in the large space.

"Did you pull a muscle?" the instructor asked as she came to Raina's side.

"No, this is something...different," she replied as a tear fell from her eye. "I feel like I'm dying."

"Tell the manager to call 911!" the teacher yelled to one of the male students in the front row. The man ran from the room to find Mara while the rest of the class gathered around Raina. Her chest began to rise and fall sporadically, sending the small group into a panic.

"She's convulsing or maybe having an asthma attack," one woman suggested.

"No, I don't think so. My son's asthma attacks don't look like this," another student offered.

"What do we do?" another woman asked. "Should we prop her head up?

"I don't think we can do anything but wait for the ambulance, unless we have a doctor in the class this morning?" Winnie asked hopefully.

Heads shook all around. "We should get her some water in case it's dehydration," someone suggested, but no one moved to make it happen.

The manager came into the room and rushed to Raina's side. "I called 911 and they said they'd send an ambulance as soon as possible!" she told her, but Raina's breathing had now slowed to a point of imperceptibility. Moments later, sirens rang outside. All but one of the students left the room, following the manager to the front of the studio.

"Look, there's an ambulance across the street!" Mara exclaimed. It had pulled to the curb but instead of coming to the yoga studio, two EMTs emerged from the back of the vehicle and rushed into a restaurant.

"That's odd. Maybe they have our address wrong?" Mara queried. A few minutes passed before the medical team burst through the front door of the eatery with a bloody body on their stretcher.

"That's a lot of blood," one of the female students said as she covered her mouth to keep from gagging.

"I'm going to run over there. Maybe we can borrow one of them," Mara announced. But before she could get out the front door, a scream came from the yoga studio.

What the class saw when they returned to the room was something that no one was expecting; Raina had regained mobility and she was ripping the body of another yogi to pieces. Gasps and then screams escaped the mouths of the class.

"Yeah, that definitely isn't dehydration," one of the students said.

Raina stopped eating the flesh of the unfortunate student and turned her head to the noise of the others. She ran at them, leaving a trail of perfect bloody footprints on the wooden floor as she did.

Michelle Kilmer and Rebecca Hansen

TERRIFYING FINDINGS

Martin Groveman, the county Medical Examiner, was having a productive day. His first autopsy had been an easy one; a domestic dispute had turned ugly and the wife of the victim shot him in the head. The second one was another gunshot victim, this time an elderly woman shot by her neighbor, the third body was more puzzling.

The man on the steel table before him had a unique story; Martin was already convinced of that. He just wasn't sure of the details yet, as partway through the internal examination, the sheriff, Bill Deen, had let himself into the mortuary.

"What can you tell me?" the sheriff asked.

"He's dead, Bill," Martin answered with a half-smile.

"That some kind of morgue humor?" Bill asked without smiling back.

"Without a little fun, this job is just no fun at all," Martin answered truthfully. "But I did find out something you'll be interested to know."

"Oh yeah?" Bill asked as he leaned a hip against the morgue table and folded his arms over his chest.

"He wasn't in the water very long at all. The start of decomposition happened on land, not in the lake."

"Are you telling me someone dumped his body there? It'd be a bit hard to move his deadweight," the sheriff surmised as he pointed to the remains on the table. He'd been on the boat when the diver located the body and a specialized team recovered him. "Whoever killed and moved this guy must have left a trail. A drag path or something."

"Another interesting thing that I found, he was in perfect condition when he died; with the body of an athlete and the internal health to match. Absolutely no trauma that suggests foul play. He had one open wound, a small mark that looked like a bite on his back. Nothing else," Martin added.

"A bite mark? We'd usually find something like that on the perpetrator; made by the victim in an attempt to end the attack." Bill furrowed his brow and stroked his mustache, deep in thought.

"There may be brain trauma that I can't see. I still need to examine his head internally. So, maybe someone did kill him."

"Why did you call me here before finishing the autopsy, Martin?" the sheriff asked with a shake of his head.

"I didn't call you, Bill. You showed up, remember?" Martin reminded him.

Bill couldn't quite remember. They'd been getting very strange phone calls at dispatch all day and there was a calm-before-the-storm type feeling in the air that really threw him off.

"You're right, I did just come. Sorry 'bout that. Give me a call when you know more." Bill extended a hand to shake but Martin was still wearing dirty gloves. Bill tipped his hat to the medical examiner instead and left the building.

Martin had already pulled away the skin and soft tissues from the top of the head, exposing the man's skull, just before Bill had arrived. Ready to pick up where he left off, he pulled down a large plastic mask to protect his face and picked up the Stryker saw. Martin placed the vibrating blade to the man's skull and made a circle around the entire diameter. Once the cutting was complete he gently lifted away the top of the skull and set it aside.

He could tell without even removing the brain that it had suffered some form of blunt trauma but the injury looked recent and there was no bleeding around the impact area.

"This doesn't make sense," Martin said, fogging up his mask for a moment. He ripped the gloves from his hands and, with the mask still covering his face, looked through the list of numbers by the telephone attached to the morgue wall. There had to be a specialist somewhere that could explain what he was seeing, he just didn't know whom to call.

Michelle Kilmer and Rebecca Hansen

WHAT THE CAT DRAGGED IN

He was on a hunt for the annoying bird that always interrupted his afternoon nap. Last he'd seen the stupid thing, it was sitting on the fence mocking his two-inch long fur and his slowness. He'd hissed at the creature and it had taken to the sky like it always did when it felt threatened. That was yesterday.

Today he couldn't find it anywhere in the backyard that he shared with his owner; the shriveled human that smelled like tuna fish and death. He spent all morning searching for the bird to no avail. *Maybe on the other side*, the feline thought. He approached the back fence and found the hole that led to a long alley behind the houses.

Usually, others of his kind could be found wandering here, but the air felt different. He smelled blood and decided to follow the trail. He hoped that he'd find a dead canine at the end of it. *The terrier,* the cat dreamed. He hated everything about that dog; the way it looked, the way it sounded, the smell of its breath and its stupid name: Teri. All of the dogs in the neighborhood were idiots, save for the white one with black spots. That dog knew more than he let on.

The cat followed the trail of blood down the alley, winding through garbage bins and on and off of the hard surface of the road and the grass that lined it. The blood took him through the back gate of a neighboring house. His sensitive nose was overloaded by the smell that hung over the yard. Animal bodies littered the overgrown lawn, gutted and left to rot in the sun.

He slowly walked through the yard, toward the deck where he could get a better view of the carnage. From there he could see the tiny body of the stupid bird and, to his surprise, the large body of the smart Dalmatian. Something had eaten them.

The strong scent of death had disabled his ability to smell danger as it approached from behind. He heard the creak of a board on the deck but could not break into a run for hands had already gripped his body. The cat struggled and managed to rotate within the clutches and secure his teeth around an arm. He bit down as hard as he could and dug his claws into whatever skin they hit. The hands instantly released him but his mouth tasted horrible, as though he'd eaten something that had been sitting for weeks at the bottom of a trashcan.

He ran back up the alley and scurried through the hole in the fence that took him to the safety of his own backyard. No matter how many times he tried to, he couldn't really clean his tongue and now his fur smelled like decay as well.

The cat approached the backdoor of his human's house and cried out loudly. Within moments the elderly woman let him inside.

"You smell disgusting!" she told the cat, holding her nose. "Let mommy give you a bath." The old woman plugged the kitchen sink and filled it with lukewarm water. She picked up the cat and dropped him in the liquid.

The cat hated baths almost as much as he hated Teri and more than he hated smelling like death. He jumped from the water and onto the woman's chest, nearly knocking her down. She gripped him but he clawed his way out of her arms.

"Ow! What a bad cat you are! Where did you learn manners like that?" She looked at her thin arms and the wounds he'd left on them. Her cat was making horrible noises on the kitchen floor, like he was crying. She comforted and towel-dried him as much as he would allow.

"Who loves her kitty? I do. Yes I do love you my big kitty," Evelyn Berry cooed as she scratched the underside of her Persian's tiny chin. The cat had forgiven her for the attempted bath and now purred heavily and rubbed his face against her wrinkled hand. "I'd be all alone without you Blue Berry."

In cat years, Blue was as close to death as Evelyn herself was. At eighty-four she was lucky to still be living without assistance from either a nurse or an oxygen tank, let alone still living. She was mobile enough to do her household work and bathe but she had to utilize a few delivery services to get what she needed. Her legs simply wouldn't survive a trek through the grocery store.

Today she was expecting her groceries from a local food delivery service. She sat in her living room, the television blared the noises of a game show.

"Buy a vowel!" Evelyn yelled at the woman on the screen. Blue Berry, who had settled his fluffy self down on her lap, jumped in shock from his owner's outburst. "It's ok, Blue. Mommy just got excited."

"Are there any G's?" the female contestant asked the show's host. A buzzer rang out signaling that no 'G's' existed on the board.

"I told you to buy a vowel," Evelyn scoffed, petting her cat's head calmly.

Ding dong

The doorbell rang, sending Evelyn's cat flying off of her lap and scratching her legs in the jump. He ran to hide under the unused dining room table.

"Such a scared-y cat! I'm coming," Evelyn said as she slowly shuffled to open the front door. On the other side stood a man with a hand truck that was stacked to its top with boxes of food; his work shirt embroidered with the logo of the company he worked for along with his name.

"Come in, Paul. The kitchen is straight back, end of the hall." Evelyn pointed behind her and let the man by.

"I can bring it in but you'll have to unpack the boxes yourself. Company policy," the man said firmly as he walked to the end of the hall. He followed company policy, especially if someone read his name off his shirt.

"Oh, well, the other delivery man puts it away for me. I'm not very capable," Evelyn lied because she wanted to get back to watching the game show. The contestants were about to solve the puzzle.

"I'm not supposed to and I'm really not feeling well, ma'am," he said truthfully.

"Won't you help out a senior citizen, just this once?" she pouted with extra frailty in her voice.

He looked at the boxes and guessed that it wouldn't take him more than ten extra minutes to help her. Old women always had such a helplessness about them that cut through his stickler ways.

"Alright," he complied, "but you can't say I did."

"Thank you!" Evelyn smiled. She left him in the kitchen, shut the front door and made her way back to her chair in front of the television. Shortly after she sat down, the deliveryman came into the living room, a can of soup in his hand.

"Where'd you like the soups?" he asked Evelyn.

"Second cupboard in on the left of the sink," she said without looking in his direction.

He returned to the kitchen and found a cat investigating the open cardboard boxes on the floor. "Are you looking for food little dude?" he asked the cat, assuming it was male and hungry. He bent down to pet the friendly-looking cat and it swung a paw at him, its claws cutting shallow scratches in his palm. "You are *not* friendly at all!"

The pain in his hand reminded him of the overall crappy feeling his whole body felt. His head hurt and a layer of perspiration covered his body. He was sure at this point that he had the flu. *Hopefully the old lady doesn't get sick from me*, he thought. *Better hurry up and get out of here.* He finished unpacking the groceries and went back to the living room.

"Ma'am? I'm all done in there. I'm heading out," he said to the woman, but he could only see the top of her thinning hair above the high back of her chair. She didn't answer.

"Ma'am?" the man asked again. He moved slowly around her chair, terrified that he was about to find a body. When he came to face her it looked like she was in fact dead. He put a finger on her shoulder, more of a prod than a tap and she sprang up from her chair.

"Oh my!" she yelled. "You frightened me! I must have fallen asleep."

Paul had fallen back toward the television and caught himself on his injured hand. "Ahh!" he called out as he pulled his hand close to his body and clutched the scratch.

"Are you ok?" the old woman asked. "What's happened to your hand?"

"Your cat, it scratched me when I tried to pet it," the man explained.

"I'm sorry about that. I don't know what's gotten into him today. He hurt me too," she apologized, showing him her own scratches. "You make sure you clean that! Cat scratches can get really nasty if you don't."

"I'll be sure to. Have a good day," he said.

The old woman followed him to the door and watched him walk back to his still-running truck.

"He doesn't look so good," she said to Blue Berry who had joined her at the door.

The cat looked up at his human. The old woman's skin color had diminished to a deathly pallor. She didn't look too good either.

Michelle Kilmer and Rebecca Hansen

THE PRICE OF CONVENIENCE

After the healthiest snack he could find at a mini mart — a snack pack of apples and grapes — Paul was back to his delivery route. His health had not improved and he was looking forward to finishing early. When he checked his clipboard for his final stop, he felt like going home immediately instead: it was Thea Mathes.

"I have to get rid of this route," Paul said to himself as he pulled his vehicle to the curb. Before he had even loaded his hand truck with her groceries, Thea was at her window watching his every move.

Even if Paul could forget about this crazy woman, her doormat would remind him whose house he was at. It read

"Wipe your feet three times before you hit the chime!" As he did, he could swear that Thea was counting. *What would you do if I only wiped once?* He wanted to ask her.

Once his feet were clean she allowed him in. The entry hall was long and Thea had installed a large hand sanitizer dispenser on either end. She pointed to the one closest to the front door.

"I have gloves on!" Paul protested.

"I saw you blow your nose out there, Paul. What's wrong? Are you sick? You know I don't allow sick people into my house," Thea said nervously.

"No, I'm fine," Paul lied. "I just had a tickle in my nose. It's from all the cardboard boxes."

"Gloves off, sanitizer on." Thea crossed her arms and stood watch until he'd done as she asked.

"Ok, I smell like I've been drinking on the job now. Can I finish this up?" He nodded in the direction of the kitchen.

"All right, but if I hear so much as a sniffle from you, you're out and I'm calling your manager," Thea declared. "It is a biological hazard to be sending sick people all over the city."

He pushed his hand truck down the hall, eyeing the second hand sanitizer dispenser as he passed by. "Hey Thea, this one's running a little low," he snickered.

Thea appeared immediately with a refill bag but was disappointed to find that Paul had lied. "I knew I'd just refilled that one! Public health is not a joke, Paul!"

Upon hearing his name used so casually once again from the mouth of a near stranger he became more irritated. "New company policy," he said to himself in the kitchen, "no wearing nametags in crazy people's houses."

Back near the front door, Thea was on her hands and knees wiping the wood floor where the hand truck had rolled with a cloth and a disinfectant spray. "Paul, I can't allow you to bring that cart in here again. It tracks too much dirt."

Her voice was sounding distant to him and his balance was wavering again, but with more intensity. Paul moved quickly to unload the boxes. This was more than a cold, possibly the flu. He pushed his hand truck into the hall and quickly slipped on a wet puddle of the spray that Thea had laid down. His head hit the floor with a *thud*.

"Oh my word!" Thea yelled and rushed to his side. His eyes were closed. "Paul! Paul, wakeup!" She shook his shoulders and gingerly grabbed his chin and moved his face side to side in an attempt to rouse him. She put her face close to his chest. He wasn't breathing and she could hear no heart beat.

Thea stood up and ran to the dispenser on the wall. She filled her hand with a small pool of the sanitizing goo. She smeared some around his mouth and on his lips and for good measure, smeared some on her own face. "Ok, Thea. As soon as he starts breathing you can stop," she comforted herself.

She checked again with the hope that he had started to breathe on his own, but he hadn't. Thea leaned toward Paul's face; her lips approached his slightly parted set.

Maybe it was the touch of skin on skin or just part of the reanimation process but as soon as she'd made contact, Paul returned to life. Thea screamed as his arms gripped her in a hug and he bit her lip.

With a strength she didn't know she had, Thea struggled free of his hold, opened her front door and ran from her house.

This time Thea was absolutely certain that something was wrong with her. Others had called her a hypochondriac in the past, but this was different. A man had drawn her blood with his mouth, a mouth that had been god knows where.

Two years prior she had a cancer scare, that no one else (not even the doctor!) thought was real. She had the weird looking mole removed just to make sure. Seven months ago she suffered severe burns to her lower legs, brought on by a close call with spontaneous combustion. The paramedics told her she had been sitting to close to a space heater. In between those two major incidents she was sick all of the time with any number of sneezes and sniffles that were floating around the neighborhood. That is why she had the dispensers installed and why she carried facemasks in her purse.

Blood ran from her cut lip and she was panting heavily after running three blocks. *I must look insane*, she thought. She pulled one of the masks from her purse and put it on. It would at least cover the wound; whether it made her look more psychotic she didn't care.

She neared the police station but kept walking. Before she could report the attack something had to be done to protect her body. There was a drug store just a few more blocks down the road; she could get what she needed there.

The door glided open for Thea and an employee in a red vest immediately greeted her.

"Can I help you find anything?" he chimed.

Thea felt she couldn't answer the question. Small talk would only allow the disease to spread faster through her body. Ignoring him, she grabbed a cart and moved with purpose to the personal health and hygiene aisle. She watched him out of the corner of her eye. When she was certain he'd moved on, she started chugging bottles of cough syrup.

Next, Thea picked up a bag of cough drops, ripped it open and unwrapped no less than ten of the herbal lozenges. She put the entire handful in her mouth and dropped the wrappers to the floor.

A security guard appeared at the end of the aisle. The man was bulky and an entire foot taller than Thea. He walked confidently but slowly toward her.

"Ma'am, I need you to put the merchandise down and follow me to the office," the guard calmly stated. Thea looked up at him in terror and shook her head in declination.

"I haf ta be helfy!" she cried out, cough drops spilling from her overstuffed mouth. "Healthy!" she yelled more clearly, collapsing to the ground amid the scattered lozenges, wrappers and empty plastic bottles.

The guard mumbled something into a radio he'd unclipped from his belt. Without warning he grabbed Thea and escorted her to the office. Thea was made to sit at the worn, Formica-topped table in the middle of the room while the guard called the police.

"Hi, uh, non-emergency. Yeah, I'd like to report a theft. Yes, the suspect is in custody. Yes, that's the address. Ok, thank you," the guard said into the office phone. He hung up and turned to face Thea. "The police are on their way."

Out in the drugstore, a manager and employee surveyed the scene of the crime. "Stanley, grab some gloves from the sales floor and clean these up," the manager directed as he nudged one of the sticky lozenges near his left foot. "And take this cart back to the front."

The employee did as he was told. With gloves hugging his hands he picked up the discarded cough drops and then found a mop to get rid of the tack they'd left on the floor. Just as he put the bucket and mop away, the police arrived to escort the woman to jail. He followed behind them, pushing the cart back to the front.

She struggled against the handcuffs and yelled at the policemen to wipe off the backseat before putting her into the car.

FREE CANDY

"This isn't preschool, mommy."

"I know. Mommy forgot to pack you something to share for snack time. We'll go to preschool next, Maia," Annette explained.

She pulled her station wagon into the drugstore parking lot. After parking, she walked to the back door to help her daughter out of the car.

As they crossed the lot to the entrance, Annette noticed a police cruiser parked parallel with the curb in front of the store. *Stupid shoplifting kids*, she thought. But, as they walked into the store, two cops staggered by with the struggling culprit in their arms. Annette was surprised to see that it was a middle-aged woman with something red smeared on her face.

"Do you need a cart, ma'am?" a sales person asked as he approached, pushing one.

"Do you want to walk like a big girl, or ride in the cart?" Annette asked Maia, though she knew what her daughter's answer would be.

"Cart!" Maia screamed a bit too excitedly.

"Inside voice," Annette calmly reminded her daughter as she accepted the cart and lifted Maia into the child seat.

Annette walked aimlessly around the aisles. She maneuvered around a 'caution, wet floor' sign near the Band-Aids. "Hmm, what happened here?" she thought aloud.

"Something got spill-ded," Maia answered.

Annette smiled and focused on finding shareable foods. In the snack section she quickly passed by the pretzels because every other mom always brought them. Coming up with nothing suitable, she went to the refrigerated section to pick up some yogurts.

While Annette left the cart to hold open the door to the cooler, Maia found something stuck to the child seat next to her. It was red and round and looked like candy. "Mommy, can I have this?" Maia asked with the sticky cough drop already in her fingers and nearing her mouth. But Annette couldn't hear her daughter over the noise of the refrigerator, especially since the yogurt hadn't been restocked, forcing her to climb halfway inside to reach anything.

Maia put the cough drop in her mouth and was happily sucking away on it when Annette returned to the cart.

"What's in your mouth?" Annette asked.

"Candy," Maia said quietly.

Annette held out her hand and Maia knew that meant she had to spit it out. The cough drop fell onto Annette's hand. She searched her purse for a tissue to wrap it in but had to settle for a gum wrapper that barely encased it.

"Where'd you find it?" Annette asked, but she didn't really want to know the answer. Kids were always putting objects in their mouths, no matter how dirty they appeared to be.

"Here," Maia touched a tiny finger to the seat. Her finger stuck a little to the residue as she pulled it away.

"Uuugh," Annette moaned. "What have I told you about eating things?"

"Ask mommy first," Maia recited. "I did."

"Well Mommy has to hear you ask the question and she has to answer you, ok?"

Maia nodded and Annette pushed the cart to the checkout lanes.

"Just the yogurt for you, ma'am?" the sales person asked from behind the register.

Annette nodded and smiled. She didn't want to sound rude so she said as politely as she could, "Do the shopping carts ever get cleaned?"

Stanley wasn't sure so he thought for a second and replied, "I could ask my manager, if you like?"

"No, that's ok. She's late for preschool. Could you throw this away for me though? My daughter found it in the cart and put it in her mouth." Annette handed him the partially wrapped cough drop.

"Oh, I'm so sorry about that! Sure thing. Have a good day, ma'am." Stanley smiled his best smile as the woman and her child left the store. He looked down at what she'd given him. He could see the red of the cough drop peeking out through the silver of the gum wrapper.

"I sure hope that crazy lady wasn't sick or anything. That'll be a lawsuit right there."

LOCKED UP

"Stand away from the bars," Officer Bo Barrett ordered the six men locked in the station's only holding cell. He'd finished booking Thea Mathes for theft and resisting arrest. She would spend the night in jail and have to go to court if the drugstore's manager decided to press charges.

"Yeah, a new friend!" a drunk man yelled as Thea was pushed into the cell. Her legs were weak and she fell to the cement floor. Another man, less drunk but more frightening looking, approached her and helped her to her feet. He could see the skin around her mouth was stained a cherry red and she smelled strongly of alcohol.

"You had a bit too much to drink, like this guy," he said pointing to the heckler. "Maybe you should take the bench."

Thea allowed the man to walk her to a long, wooden seat that spanned the back wall of the cell. Too ill to care about the grime, she lay down and closed her eyes. The men around her talked as she drifted in and out of consciousness.

"She's not too bad looking," one man commented.

"Yeah but she can't hold her liquor," said another.

"Think she'll give me her number when she wakes up?" the drunk man asked loudly.

"You don't want to call her. She'll drink all your booze," a fourth man pointed out.

"Yer right," the drunk replied.

Things in the cell quieted down until Thea started to die. She began kicking her legs wildly, forcing the men on the bench beyond them to get out of the way.

"What's wrong with her?" the drunk slurred.

"She's just dreaming. Running from something," another man suggested.

"Ha! The police," a third man said, which sent chuckles around the cell.

Thea's movement stopped as abruptly as it started. Her body lay prone on the bench for sometime as the men around her shared stories and the toilet.

Officer Barrett walked by the cell to check on its occupants. He noticed that Thea was as still as a corpse.

"She doesn't look right. Did one of you do something to her?" he asked accusingly.

A gangbanger approached the bars, his face full of anger. "Are you calling me a murderer?" he asked the cop.

"No, I'm not. But, since you said the word, I'm volunteering you to check on her. Go give her a shake, make sure she's ok." The officer folded his arms on his chest and waited for the thug to do as he was told.

"Shit, I'm not touching that ho. She jus' came in off da street!" he replied and returned to sitting on the floor against one of the cell's walls.

The officer was searching his keys to open the cell door when Thea rose from the bench. She moved slowly and her face was no longer relaxed. Her cough syrup stained lips were parted, showing equally reddened teeth.

"Yo, Barrett," the gangbanger said, "she look ok to me."

Officer Barrett looked away from his keys and at the woman. Her arms hung slack at her sides and she was drooling. "She still doesn't look right," he said.

The drunkest of the men approached her and touched her shoulder. "Lady," he said. Thea turned toward him and pounced. The inebriated man fell to the floor with Thea on top of him, her teeth tearing flesh from his neck.

"Ms. Mathes, step away from him. Put your hands on your head!" Bo yelled as he stuck his baton between the bars, attempting to get her attention. He put his baton away and pulled out his gun but she ignored the firearm and continued to make a meal of the prisoner. The men inside the cell had a moment of shock before realizing that they too might be in danger. The men started begging the officer to open the cell.

"Let us out!" they yelled, but Bo didn't move for his key ring. He couldn't allow six men and a deranged woman to wander the halls of the station.

"I'll get some help, just stay away from her!" he directed.

The five remaining men were huddled in the corner opposite the blood bath, fighting to be closest to the wall and furthest from Thea.

"She ain't drunk. I think it's that *bath salts* shit," one of the men said quietly. He didn't want to attract Thea's attention.

"I don't care what it is, I'm not going near it," another commented.

"That was almost *my* neck," the gangbanger reflected.

Just as Thea started to move away from the carnage she'd made of the drunkard and toward the huddled men, Bo returned with two more officers. One of them immediately drew his gun and shot her in the head.

"What the fuck?" Bo yelled.

"You should have done that in the first place, rookie. She just attacked a man and you let her," the cop explained, shaking his head.

"I've never seen someone eat another person. They didn't train for this in the academy."

"It's called thinking on your feet; making fast decisions. They taught you THAT."

"What are we going to do with these bodies?" Bo asked.

"Yeah man, get them out of here. This is inhumane, leaving them in here with us," one of the prisoners said.

"We can't move them until the medical examiner comes," the cop replied. "I'll go call him. Bo, keep an eye on things here until I get back."

The angry gangbanger stepped forward. "What choo think man, think I'm gonna defile a corpse?"

"We don't think anything about you, Darnell," Bo retorted.

"That's emotional police brutality, man!" Darnell walked up to the corpse of the drunkard and leaned close to get a better view of his wounds. "She really chewed his neck up good!" He touched a finger to the man's blood-covered neck.

"Don't touch the body. The man could have AIDS," Bo told him.

"He don't have shit no more," Darnell said as he pulled his gore-covered finger from the wound and wiped it on the dead man's shirt.

Michelle Kilmer and Rebecca Hansen

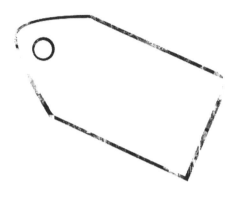

POST MORTEM

With all the bodies piling up, it was proving to be an eventful day for Dr. Martin Groveman, especially now that he had a body with a bullet from a policeman's handgun in its head.

He had a hard time believing the officers' story but they insisted that they had no other choice in the matter than to shoot the woman before she did any further damage. They claimed she had mostly decapitated a man with her teeth and nothing else.

"The head nearly severed from the body...from a supposed bite wound? Far fetched," he mumbled as he unzipped the body bag of the executed woman. "Looks like you had a hell of a day, honey. Let's get you opened up and have a look at your insides."

Swesh! A noise came from the direction of the other body bag that had been picked up at the jail.

"Ladies first," Martin said, often speaking to the dead as if they were still living. "You're just going to have to wait in line, mister."

Whoosh! More noise came from the corner of the room.

"Looks like we've got a live one over there," he joked to himself as he examined the woman's body for injuries.

Picking up his voice recorder he documented his observations. "The damage sustained appears only to be to the face. A single bullet has entered into the forehead, no exit wound. A two-inch gash is present on the bottom lip. The lower half of the face is a deep cherry red; officers stated it was a mixture of cough syrup and blood. I'm taking a sample for analysis."

He cleaned off what he could from her face to better view the lip wound and then proceeded with the autopsy, making a long incision from the top of her chest down to her lower abdomen. "It's a good day for a little internal investigation," the examiner chuckled.

Whish! SWOOSH! The noise grew suddenly, much louder than before.

"Oh you found that funny did you? Nice to get some reaction, the crowd's usually *dead* in here," he joked as he turned toward the table where the body of the man lay. A small movement from the lower portion of the bag made it seem as though a leg had shifted, almost in reaction to the doctors voice.

"If you're alive in there then it's got to be some sort of miracle! This lady put a pretty big hole in your neck," he said as he pointed back toward the woman. "Maybe you can tell me what you did to piss her off so much? That would make my job a whole lot easier. You know, 'case closed' easier."

The bag started wiggling and areas of it poked out where the man's elbows and knees bent with each jagged movement. Seeing this, the doctor became worried that the man was in fact alive and most likely panicking from being zipped in a large plastic bag. *How could he be alive?* The doctor thought to himself as he walked closer to the table.

Martin opened the bag about half way to allow the man to breathe but was not prepared for what he saw looking back at him. The man sat up and stared blankly at him, his body a deathly bluish-white and his head set crookedly on what was left of his neck.

"Eek," Martin jumped as he screamed. "You are most definitely *not* alive." Not knowing what to do, he pinned the man down, zipped up the bag and took a few steps back. "Well, this complicates things," he said as walked to the phone mounted on the wall to dial the sheriff's number. "Better see what Bill has to say about this!"

The phone rang twice before it was answered. "King County Sheriff's office, this is SusAnna, how may I direct your call?"

"Um, yes, this is Martin Groveman from the Medical Examiner's office. I uh…have a…uh…situation over here," he said gesturing to the slithering body bag as if the receptionist was standing next to him.

"A situation, at the morgue?" she laughed. "Did someone come back to life or something?"

"Well *YES*, but I'd feel more comfortable talking to Bill about this."

"Is this some sort of joke, Mr. Groveman?"

"NO, I wish it were. Now, can I please talk to the sheriff?" Martin asked, frustration growing in his voice.

"Yes sir, sorry, right away. Please, hold."

SOMETHING TO SHARE

"Alright! Now that all of our friends are here we can get started! Does everyone have their buddies?" Veronica Peters asked, as she looked around the room at the bouncy, messy-haired heads of ten 4-year-olds.

"Yes," the group of preschoolers responded as they calmed down and sought to hold their buddy's hand.

It gave Veronica the creeps when all the kids answered at the same time, especially when they did it holding hands. *All Village of the Damned like,* she thought. She was a non-traditional teacher and an even more non-traditional person outside of school, preferring the company of animals to people and spending hours reading about witchcraft and serial killers. If the parents of the preschoolers knew anything about her personal interests, they wouldn't bring their kids to her. She snapped a smile back on her face. "Let's all sit on the center rug and we can start sharing time. Does anyone have something they'd like to share?" she asked.

Most of the children were shy but she could always count on one or two of them to eat up the time by describing a toy they had lost or an animal they had seen at the zoo. A small hand shot into the air. "Danny, go ahead," Veronica invited him to speak.

"My doggy runned away," he said as he picked his nose. He then sat down, offering no more information on the absent pooch.

"I'm sorry to hear that. That's sad, isn't it?" she asked the other children. Many nodded in agreement. One girl, who was rather emotional on most days, started crying.

"It's ok," her buddy said to her.

"Does anyone else have something to share with their friends?" Veronica asked.

Without raising her hand, Maia stood up and started talking. "A lady got rested from the yogurt store."

"Miss Maia, we don't talk until we raise our hand and get called on, right?" Veronica gently reminded her, though she had little patience for Maia as the little girl often ignored rules. "You can spend five minutes in time out while everyone else plays."

Maia stomped to the time out corner while the other children scattered to different learning tables around the room. After five minutes, Veronica retrieved her.

"Go ahead and join the others," Veronica said as she watched the girl slowly rise and retreat to the empty finger painting station.

After thirty minutes of activities, Veronica called the children back to the center rug. "Today we are going to continue learning about animals. Does everyone remember the animals they chose yesterday?"

The children nodded.

"When I say 'go' I want everyone to pretend to be their animal. You can walk like your animal and make noises like it. Now, go!"

The children milled about on the center rug and slowly traveled to all corners of the room. One of the girls had picked a pigeon, which she called a 'pig-en', after having seen them in the park. She waved her arms around excitedly. Another child, a boy, was a bear. Danny, the boy who'd lost his dog, was a lion but he was copying the movements of the bear. Maia had picked rabbit, but she hadn't moved from the center rug.

"Aren't you going to hop around like a bunny, Maia?" Veronica asked her, but the girl looked tired. "Do you want to start nap time early?"

Maia shook her head and started to gently hop around the room. After a short time she too started copying the bear child's movements. Danny saw this and became angry.

"I'M the LION!" he yelled at her.

Veronica had been watching one of the smallest girls pretend to be a goldfish, but her head instinctively whipped toward the yelling voice. "What's wrong, Danny?"

"I'm 'posed to be the lion. Not her!" he yelled and pointed at Maia, whose fingers were gnarled into pretend lion's claws.

"Let's all pretend to be our *own* animals, children," Veronica said calmly as she looked at the clock on the wall. "Well, time's up anyway. Who wants a nap?" *I know I do,* she thought. She quickly laid out ten blue mats on the floor and watched as the kids picked one and closed their eyes. Veronica turned down the lights and exited the room into an inner hallway of the small building to find coffee.

Being so young, Maia didn't notice the changes her ill body was undergoing as she napped. She was sweating but goose bumps crawled along her arms. She tossed and turned until her body went numb and her breathing stopped.

Naptime was usually fifteen to thirty minutes depending on how long it took Veronica to get rid of her daily headache. Ten minutes into her midday peace she heard a scream from the classroom. She was about to open the door but Danny burst through it, crying.

"What's wrong?" Veronica asked him. "Did you have a bad dream?"

"I'M THE LION!" he yelled.

"I know you're the lion, Danny. Is Maia still pretending?" Veronica asked. Sometimes the children didn't go to sleep during naptime, instead choosing to wander the classroom and disrupt the others. The boy nodded his head and lifted his small arm to show her what Maia had done.

"The lion bited me!" he cried as the other children began screaming.

"Go to the first aid box by the sink, ok?" Veronica directed him as she opened the door to the classroom and turned the lights back on. There were a couple of children still lying on the mats, motionless. The rest of the class had sought refuge underneath the activity tables. Maia stood with one of the goldfish girl's arms in her hands.

"Maia, time out right now!" Veronica yelled at the girl.

At the sound of the teacher's loud voice, Maia started toward her. Her teeth were bared and she still held her hands out in front of her like lion's claws.

"Stop this!" Veronica screamed but Maia kept moving in her direction. The teacher knew she could overpower the child if she needed to but she feared a lawsuit from the parents. Indecision left her when Maia's tiny teeth bit down on her arm. Veronica picked up the girl and walked to the bathroom. She set Maia down inside the small room and closed the door as quickly as she could. She could hear the child clawing at the wood of the door but she felt nothing for her. Maia's lack of respect for her authority had gone on too long.

"Rose, can you bring me my purse?" she asked the goldfish girl. Dutifully, the child brought it to her. She pulled her cell phone out of the bag and with trembling fingers she found the contact listing for Maia's mom.

"Hi, Annette," Veronica said when the familiar voice answered on the other end. "You'll have to pick up Maia. I'm not sure if she's sick or something but she is acting very strange. She bit some of the other kids and then me...No, I haven't called any of the other parents yet...No, I can't put her on the phone. She's in the bathroom and I'm not letting her out until you get here...I told you, she attacked us...I don't know what's wrong! I'm not a psychologist. Please, just come get her." Veronica hung up and started down the list of other parents.

"Hi, Barry. Can you come back to the preschool and pick up Danny? I don't want you to be alarmed but another child bit him on his forearm...No, no, he'll be fine. It isn't bad at all."

(UN) PLANNED OUTING

It was a typical day at the Riverwood Senior Care Home, a full service hospice center in the city. Albert Wilson, clad in only a bathrobe sat in his small, sparsely decorated room drifting between reality and fiction.

"Just PICK a dress! We're going to be late for the show," he screamed at the corner of his room where his mind told him his wife was standing. The reality was that she'd never been to his room as she had passed on some 15 years prior.

One of the nurses poked her head in the doorway, "You have plenty of time before the evening movie, Mr. Wilson."

"Don't tell my wife that, she's already slower than molasses!" Albert whispered, leaning slightly forward in his chair.

In recent years Albert's dementia had forced him into 24-hour care mostly due to his increasingly lucid hallucinations and his penchant for wandering from the safety of his own home. His overall health had also started to deteriorate and today was no exception. When he'd awoken that morning, his breath was short and his chest tight. The afternoon showed no improvement but he wasn't about to mention it to the nurse and miss the movie. The beeping machines they'd hook him to wouldn't be allowed in either.

"I'll be coming around with your vitamins in a few hours," the nurse said. Albert nodded but said nothing in response so she continued on her rounds.

He had just decided to get dressed when pain came rippling through his chest. His wife came to his side and ran her fingers through his thinning hair. He closed his eyes as the agony was quickly replaced by comfort and warmth. She said softly, "I've picked a dress and the show's about to start. It's time to go." His body relaxed in the chair and he drew his final breath.

Albert's body shuddered. As quickly as he had passed he rose again. His wife no longer by his side, no pain or discomfort, no feelings to be had; he sat lifeless in the chair unknowing of his new existence.

A deliveryman arrived at the care home, propping a side door open. He pushed a hand truck, filled with large boxes of canned goods and other menu item ingredients, down the long corridor past the hall leading to the resident rooms. The squeaking of the lower left wheel echoed off the walls.

The noise drew Albert's attention, his body directing him out of the chair and out the cracked door of his room. He reached the end of the hall but his ears heard nothing more of the noise. Another sense took over, his eyes catching the light from outside. He veered left and headed for the open door.

The woods around the facility were a dense and seemingly un-passable mix of blackberry bushes and large, thick fir trees. Unconcerned, he cut a stumbling path through the thicket with no set destination. After some time he reached the edge of the forest, naked and covered in small scratches. His robe sat snagged on a thorny branch a few yards behind him. Ahead lay a short and narrow dirt path set between two houses and the fences on either side lead him straight into the street.

Michelle Kilmer and Rebecca Hansen

CAUGHT IN THE NUDE

The station wagon's engine had just cooled down from its earlier trip to the drug store and preschool. Annette, though worried about Maia's behavior and what sounded like chaos at the school, allowed it to warm up again before heading out.

Deciding it would be faster, Annette took a shortcut through a large housing development. Two and three-story homes put her rambler to shame but she had no time to dwell on her living situation. The houses became a blur as she accelerated down the asphalt. She crossed her fingers hoping that all the children in the neighborhood were at school, safe from her maniac driving.

As if her day could not get any stranger, a naked elderly man emerged from an alley between two houses. His body was covered in wrinkles and scratches.

Annette was unsure if she could do anything to help, but instinctively hit the brakes thinking the worst thing that could happen was a nude hug from the frail old man. She pulled the car to the curb, exited and approached him slowly. "Excuse me, Sir?" she said softly while searching for another place to look, as his loose and sagging skin was hard on the eyes.

Albert turned slowly, responding to the women's voice, his arms reaching out to her.

"Oh no," Annette worried aloud, "Do you need any help? What happened to you?" She tried to distract him with questions but he continued toward her. She could see a variety of cuts and scrapes on his body, but they were bloodless and non-lethal. He appeared lost and disoriented. "Is there somewhere you belong?" she asked, eyeing a medical bracelet on his wrist.

A moan escaped from the man's throat as he grabbed her arm and brought it to his mouth. He had much more strength than his withered state suggested. He gummed relentlessly on her until she managed to slip free.

"Gross," Annette said as she scrambled for the cell phone in her pocket. "Thank God you don't have teeth!"

A sudden, sharp pain moved from her neck and into the rest of her body. She jerked to the left, away from the unknown attacker but into the arms of the naked senior citizen. Her eyes fell on what had bitten her. It was a man in a uniform, his nametag, though slightly obscured by blood, read "Paul". A small piece of flesh dangled from his mouth for a moment before disappearing down his throat. The nude man was gumming the top of her head and she struggled to get away from him. She could feel warm blood running down her neck and onto her shirt. Annette screamed loudly as her mind flashed back to the phone call she'd received from the daycare.

Her daughter had bitten someone.

Is Maia one of these things? How could that be? She wondered. Annette took a closer look at the neighborhood around her. It had descended into a chaos that she hadn't noticed as she was speeding through.

As her blood continued to drain, she felt herself growing weaker, the life slowly leaving her body. She dropped to her knees and began to crawl along the sidewalk in the direction of the preschool, creating a trail of blood behind her.

"I'll be there soon, Maia," Annette said struggling for breath, "Mommy will be there soon."

Michelle Kilmer and Rebecca Hansen

DOMESTICALLY DISTURBED

After the earlier mess, the sheriff sent Bo Barrett out on patrol. The influx of calls that day meant that no one could be seen standing around the station. Bo hated patrol, due to the growing number of officers who had died from gun violence on the job. As though a test of nerves, the first call Bo responded to involved a gun. His cruiser pulled up across the street from the address given by dispatch, an address he'd been to several times before. A man sat on the front steps of the house with a pistol in his hands.

Bo stood behind his car and said loudly, but calmly, "Mr. Hill, put the gun down, sir!"

The man shook his head and pointed to the large window next to the front door. Behind the glass stood a woman. Her face was bloody and her hands clawed at the window. "No way, you didn't see what she did to the neighbor!"

"Nothing gives you the right to beat her, Brian. Put the gun on the grass."

"Beat her? I didn't do that to her. That's the neighbor's blood, not hers! She...ate him and I'm the one who called you."

"Sir, we've been here in the past. I've seen what you can do. Making up crazy stories is only going to hurt you more."

"I'm telling you the truth, officer. I didn't touch her. Haven't you been watching the news?"

"I'm still going to need you to put the gun down."

"If I do that, she's going to eat me too! Go take a look in my neighbor's backyard. You'll see what I mean."

"I'm not leaving here until you drop the weapon. No one is going to eat you." Bo called for backup on his walkie, but the response from dispatch was that none was available. Something like that had never happened. There had *always* been backup.

A small dog barked wildly from inside the house and the woman disappeared from the window. Not a minute later, the dog yelped in pain.

"Not the fucking dog!" the man on the doorstep yelled as he jumped to his feet and threw the front door open. His wife charged from the hallway, out of the door and forced him into the yard. Her hands and face were covered in a fresh mix of blood and fur.

"Ma'am, stop right there!" Bo yelled. "Stop or I'll shoot!"

The woman was nearly on top of her husband when both he and Bo took aim and opened fire. She fell to the grass when a bullet pierced her temple.

"I told you it wasn't me this time," the man said, finally putting his gun away by tucking it into the back of his belt. "She's not the only one either. I trapped her in the house but not before she got the neighbor."

"I have to call this in and I'm going to check on the neighbor. I'll need to get a statement from you." Bo walked around the side of the house but could see no one in the neighboring backyard. His knocks on the front door went unanswered.

"He isn't there," Bo said as he rejoined the man on his front lawn. "Now, tell me what happened."

The man thought for a moment and looked around nervously. "Can we do that in your car? I don't feel safe."

"Ok, but you'll have to sit in the back and I'll need your gun," Bo told him.

The two men sat in the police cruiser. Bo listened from the front seat as Brian began to recount what had taken place.

"This sounds kind of crazy," Bo said partway through his story.

"You saw her! She wasn't right," Brian reminded him.

They were interrupted when a vehicle careened into the parked car, sending Brian's body forward and his head smashing into the bulletproof glass that separated them. Bo too was forced forward by the impact, his shoulder meeting the steering wheel with dislocating force.

"Fuck!" Bo yelled, readying himself to exit the vehicle and arrest the driver.

Brian had righted himself and turned in time to see that the street behind them was full of blood-covered people and they were heading their way. "Officer Barrett, look!" he yelled, pointing out the back window.

"Holy shit! There must be thirty people out there!" Bo said as he gently rubbed the pain in his shoulder. "I'm not sure what's going on but this is bad."

"How many bullets do you have?"

"Not enough and my shoulder's hurting bad. We can't go out there," Bo determined as the crowd of disturbed citizens gathered around the disabled vehicles, pounding on the glass.

"Are the windows shatterproof?" Brian asked hopefully.

"I think so," Bo said with uncertainty.

Brian slid down in the hard plastic backseat and gripped his handgun in his lap. Bo tried calling for backup once more, but dispatch didn't respond.

ON A BOAT

They'd struck out on the water earlier that day in a two-person paddleboat. Dressed in layered clothing and hats and gloves, the couple was prepared to spend a few hours on Green Lake. Not six and counting.

The excursion started normally with the usual pointing out of ducks on the lake, cute dogs on the path that surrounded it and staring at the sky hoping the clouds would hold their rain. But as the hours passed, stranger and stranger events began to transpire.

The ducks were frightened first. Just after midday all of the ducks from the east side of the lake burst into the sky and made a quick trip to the brushes of the north end. A similar flight was made by another group of ducks from the south end to the north and now the north side of the lake was covered in them. They paddled toward the crowd of dabbling ducks and were soon in the middle of it. Sasha stared at them and tried to count just how many they were seeing.

"Get out the bread, Sasha," Curtis urged, "while the ducks are all around us."

"I don't want to scare them," she explained. "Something already has them freaked out."

"Don't worry about it. I'm pretty sure they equate the sound of plastic to the sound of food."

"Fine! I'll do it if you take some pictures," she relented. As soon as she opened the bag for the bread, the ducks once again took to the sky. This time they all flew to a small island in the lake. "I told you!" Sasha yelled at her boyfriend.

"It wasn't the bag," Curtis said as he pointed at the shore. A man waded in the shallows there, trying to capture a remaining duck. Beyond him in the grassy area of the park, a woman in jogging attire was doing the same thing.

"Why are they chasing them?" Sasha asked.

"Don't know. But if we paddle to the island we can feed them there," Curtis suggested.

"All right," Sasha said but as she paddled she kept looking over her shoulder at the people acting strangely on the shore.

As they were feeding the ducks scattered around the island, something else disturbed their date. A woman's shrill scream and the loud barking of a dog pierced the air. Other dogs howled in response. More people started to scream.

A tiny Chihuahua darted through the tall bushes and into the lake, its leash still dangling from its collar. The dog swam aimlessly for a while until Sasha and Curtis called to it and convinced it to swim in their direction. Curtis pulled the dog from the water and wrapped it in a blanket. He could see that it had a leg wound and that the leash was saturated with what looked like blood.

"Something isn't right here," he said to himself.

"I want to go home," Sasha whined. "We can drop the dog off at a vet or something."

"All right, let's take the boat in," Curtis complied. The couple paddled back to the east side of the lake.

"Do you see that?" Curtis pointed to the floating dock between them and the shore. In the middle of it a young girl stood fully clothed, soaking wet and screaming; dozens of hands thrashed in the water.

In the boat, the dog began to bark wildly. "Shhhh," Sasha tried to calm it.

"What the hell is going on? Are those people drowning?"

"That's a lot of people to be drowning all at once."

The girl noticed the boat and began waving frantically to them. "Help me!" she shrieked.

"Paddle, Sasha!" Curtis directed.

They paddled as hard as they could to close the distance, but as they reached the people in the water, the boat started to rock. When they were close enough, the girl jumped aboard just as a single hand grabbed hold of the side of the boat. Hand after hand followed and pulled on the small watercraft, tipping it back and forth violently.

Sasha was cradling the terrified child as Curtis used an unopened wine bottle to smash the fingers until they let go. There were too many and soon the paddleboat overturned, dumping them into the water. Sasha lost the girl and tried in vain to find her. Curtis attempted to right the boat and then, when that didn't work, to swim to the floating dock.

Their struggling hands were lost in the sea of others. The small dog swam some distance before disappearing under the water as well. The infected pulled at their bodies from every side, bringing the flesh of the living to their undead lips.

OVERPREPARED

Jackson counted. Jackson always counted. Sometimes, he couldn't stop counting. "One, two, three, four, four, four, five…blankets," he marked on his daily checklist while standing in the bunker buried in his backyard. Installed by a previous owner of the home, the shelter didn't quite meet his standards but he felt lucky to have it at all.

There was a time when he would only visit the bunker monthly for inventory, but his counting had taken over and if he wasn't within its confines, he was thinking about being there. In the past week he'd found it hard to leave for the night and he had become intent on making it a comfortable, permanent home.

8' x 20' in dimension with 12" thick walls, Jackson was certain it would protect him no matter what type of apocalypse might befall mankind, especially with its small cache of specialized survival gear. He had procured:

- Assorted tin foil hats in the event of an alien invasion
- An army issue gas mask in case of nuclear war
- One inflatable raft with rain shelter (two oars) if the polar ice caps melted
- Replacement chainsaw blades for decapitating zombies
- Heavy duty bug spray and a netted hat for the plague of locusts sent by God

No one could call him underprepared.

"Three-hundred, three-hundred and one," Jackson murmured as he dug through the bucket of AA batteries. He'd collected them from the now unused items that littered his former home just five yards away.

A plus side to stockpiling was taste testing dehydrated meals; he wanted to make sure his End-Of-The-World menu was not only sustaining, but also delicious. The Chicken Vindaloo was way too spicy, the Pasta Primavera had great flavor but gave him gas, but his favorite by far was the Beef Stroganoff, of which he had bought the local outdoor store's entire stock.

One part of his mind told him to re-count the non-perishables, the other attempted to assure him that the number from yesterday was accurate. So consumed by his prepping, Jackson was now unaware of life outside and cut off from any communications aside from a CB Radio that he occasionally scanned. He had no idea of the catastrophic events unfolding a few feet above him.

"I had ten, now I have eight. Where have the others gone? Did someone get in here? *Impossible!*" He stormed around the bunker looking for the two missing knives. In fact, Jackson only ever had eight knives but he'd mixed up the flashlight list with the knives list unknowingly. Endless days of shuffling about the underground shelter seemed to cause more disarray for Jackson then any sort of real system.

After he finished his counting he checked the CB Radio to make sure it was still functioning. The dial clicked on with a gentle turn to the right and Jackson picked up the mic. "Testing one, two, one, two. This is *BunkerBronco30*, is anyone out there? Over."

"Hey Buckin' Bronco, you copy? It's *dead* out here, over," a tired voice crawled through the speaker.

"The name's *BUNKER* Bronco! I'm in a *bunker*, over."

"That's one hell of a place to be right now, over."

"Why would you say that? Over."

"I told you, it's *DEAD* out here!" the man on the line reiterated. "Why don't you tell me where your little hiding place is, Buckin' Bronco? Over."

Jackson quickly regretted having turned on the radio. There was always some abrasive jerk trying to elicit personal information from him. But he knew better than to give too much away so he turned the radio off.

"Conversation terminated," Jackson smirked.

Only seconds had passed before the solitude of the bunker was disrupted by the sound of scraping from above. Jackson moved toward the center of the room directly under an air vent, noticing light and dark shifting through the metal slats. Something was moving up there.

"Freaking raccoons," he yelled. Slipping his shoes on, he slowly made his way up the ladder to ground level. In the past the critters had caused minor damage to the vent covers and no matter how often Jackson shooed them away, they always came back.

At ground level, he saw a large raccoon positioned at the vent. Its tiny hands were covered in soil from digging frantically around it.

"Not this time you're not!" Jackson yelled at the thieving creature, causing it to lumber off toward his front yard. He kneeled to rearrange the torn up sod as a woman stumbled up behind him. Before she could reach him she fell through the open hatch of the bunker and hit the floor with a loud thud.

Fearing the raccoon had returned, Jackson jumped to his feet and began to make his way down the ladder. "Keep your dirty paws off my Beef Stroganoff!" he yelled.

Halfway down the ladder she grabbed his ankle and pulled him off, sending him crashing to the floor. As pain traveled up his leg he found enough courage to look at what he now lay next to. The woman struggled to get closer to him but her legs had broken in the fall. One side of her body was caked in blood that looked to have come from a gaping wound on her neck.

"Garrrgghhh," she growled.

"Aaaaaaare *YOU* a zooooombie?" Jackson shook having even said the Z word. He tried to stand but found his legs just as powerless as hers.

"GRRRRRGGGHHH!"

"I'll take that as a YES!" He shuttered as he pushed his back against the shelf that lined the wall of the bunker. Jackson looked at his options. His knives, the only weapons he had in the bunker, were out of reach behind her and the chainsaw blades were useless without a saw.

Michelle Kilmer and Rebecca Hansen

DO UNTO OTHERS

Maia was still locked in the bathroom and would resume her desperate attempts to free herself every time she heard a noise. Few parents had arrived to pick up their children from the preschool and Veronica was doing her best to restore sanity. She played a cd of the children's favorite songs while preparing snacks, but the students who had been bitten were suffering. She felt strange herself and couldn't wait to walk the few feet to her attached home.

Cole, one of the boys who'd been injured, dropped unexpectedly to the floor. "My legs are funny!" he yelled to Veronica.

"Can you stand up?" she asked him.

"Uh uh," the boy said sadly as he shook his head.

"Ok, well maybe you should play on the floor for now." It was hardly a solution but Veronica had no idea what to say.

Rose, Serah's mother, was the first to show up. She stood on the center carpet and looked around the room. Children were scattered about – some still on mats and some on the carpet – and there were bloodstains on the floor.

"There's more blood than I expected," Rose said weakly. Her daughter ran to her and immediately presented her wounded arm. "Oh my God! She'll need stitches!"

"I didn't want to say anything on the phone that would put you in a panic," Veronica explained.

"Where is Annette?" Rose asked with fury in her voice. "And where is that little brat of hers?"

"Calm down, Rose," Veronica had little energy left to say much more to the distressed mother.

"I WILL NOT calm down! My daughter will be scarred for life physically and emotionally and you are sitting here doing nothing!"

"I locked Maia in the bathroom and she bit me too," Veronica said defensively.

"I hope you lose your license over this. In fact, I'll make sure of it. Come on, Serah, time to find you a new preschool, after we take care of your owie." Serah followed her mother outside on unstable legs and went limp as her mother strapped her into the car seat. "Oh baby, let's get you to the hospital."

It was only twelve blocks away, but traffic was heavy on the route. Many people were attempting to take injured people to the emergency room and some of them had abandoned their vehicles. When Rose checked on Serah in the rear-view mirror, she got a shock. Her daughter's face was pale and her head hung, resting against her tiny chest.

"Serah?" Rose called to her. The little girl did not respond. With no option but to find help elsewhere, Rose turned down the next side street and away from the hospital toward the only other place she trusted: the church.

She floored the accelerator pedal, driving the minivan up the steep hill to the holy place. As she tried to feel her daughter's forehead for temperature, Serah snapped her head up and bit her mother's hand with enough force that her teeth broke the skin and sunk deep into muscle. Rose clutched her hand to stop the bleeding and lessen the pain.

"Why would you do that to Mommy?" she couldn't help but cry out. Serah looked menacingly at her and began to struggle against the straps of the child seat. A snarl, which might have been cute had the girl's mouth not been leaking blood, appeared on the girl's lips. "I'll be right back. Mommy is going to ask the pastor for help." Rose slid the van door closed and made her way around the building to the front door.

Michelle Kilmer and Rebecca Hansen

BACK STORIES OF THE DEAD

Martin was still on hold, waiting for the sheriff to take his call when a buzzer rang. It came from the back door; the one used for bringing new bodies in or sending out those ready for the funeral home. He set the phone down and reluctantly made his way to the pair of metal doors at the end of the hall.

"I didn't get any new calls and I don't really have any vacancies at the moment," he yelled, hoping whoever it was would leave. After all, it wasn't normal for someone to just show up unless they were deceased and he had personally escorted them there in his large, non-descript white van.

Something on the other side of the doors was blocking the daylight from creeping in at the floor.

Martin opened the door slowly to find what appeared to be a body wrapped in some sort of tablecloth and a note weighed down by a rock.

He picked up the note and read it aloud, "You wouldn't believe us if we told you." He flipped the paper over, looking for more information or a signature, but it was blank.

"HA! After what I've seen today, try me," he scoffed as he pulled back the fabric. "Holy shit!"

Martin ran back to the phone just in time for the sheriff to pick up the other end of the line.

"Hello? Sheriff Deen, here."

"Took you long enough, Bill! It's Martin. I need some advice," the medical examiner's voice quavered.

"I can't stay on long, make it quick! Everyone's out on calls so I'm shorthanded," Bill snapped.

"Well, I have someone who isn't quite dead trying to get out of a body bag and, no kidding, someone just dumped the body of Patrick Houlihan from First Lutheran at the back door."

"The pastor, no shit? He was a good man. What happened to him?"

"From the looks of it, and this is pure speculation, someone bludgeoned him to death. Left an anonymous, cryptic note on him too."

"The world really is going to hell," Bill sighed. "What kind of advice do you need?"

"Like I said, I have a body that is still moving and a murdered preacher. I don't know what to do."

"My advice is this: go home, walk away," the sheriff said calmly.

"You want me to leave with bodies still on the tables?"

"The government is recommending it, not me. Things are beyond control. I'm packing up to leave myself."

"We can't abandon our posts! The public is counting on us to keep doing our jobs!" Martin yelled into the phone.

"It's your call, Martin. I'm still alive and I want to stay that way. I have to go." The sheriff disconnected the call.

Martin placed the phone back on its cradle and returned to the deceased pastor's side. "I bet you're in Heaven, Pastor. Well, I *hope* you're there. Let's get your skin suit out of the cold and into the cooler." Martin dragged the body as kindly as he could, past the cherry-stained woman and the bouncing body bag, into the refrigerated room. He lifted the corpse onto a table and placed a sheet over it.

Who would bash a pastor's head in? Martin wondered, "and how are these people connected?"

Michelle Kilmer and Rebecca Hansen

BY THE BOOK

Pastor Pat didn't know he would be dead by dinnertime or that someone from his congregation would take his life. He definitely never imagined his body would be dumped at the back door of the county morgue.

Every Tuesday evening he hosted a bible study. He spent the early part of the day preparing the lesson and then he did odd jobs around the church until the class participants started arriving. Lila, the office manager, showed up earlier than normal for her shift and was running hurriedly from room to room within the church as though she was looking for something. She was hastily dressed in workout pants and an oversized t-shirt, very unlike the normally uptight professional.

"Pastor Houlihan, lock the doors and bless some more water! Demons are running loose on the street!" Lila shrieked as she searched the narthex for something to secure the front doors.

"Calm down, Lila! I've heard the news and we have nothing to fear. God unleashed this plague for a reason. We'll be safe here."

"You and I aren't sick, we can't allow anyone else in!"

"Bible Study is tonight and *everyone* is welcome in God's house," the pastor reminded her.

"No! Not today!" she shrieked as she fled deeper into the church.

Other congregation members arrived seeking safe haven. They made way to the sanctuary, many of them anxious but comforted by the wooden pews, hymnal books and stained glass they'd spent so much time with. Pat took his spot in front of the altar, but not in his usual worship attire. On Tuesdays it was jeans and sweatshirts for him. He looked out on the group of fifteen.

"I'm glad to see you're all safe. You're welcome to stay here as long as necessary. Let us pray." The pastor clasped his hands together, "Dear Lord, please protect us from this plague. Show us Your love and mercy. Look after those who have already been lost. In Your name we pray. Amen."

"Amen," the small crowd recited.

"Since there's no sermon today, you are free to pray, sing, whatever you would like. I'll be wandering around to visit with everyone." Pat stepped from the elevated stage that held the altar and walked down the center of the two rows of pews. In the corner of his eye, movement in the courtyard caught his attention. He excused himself from the group in the sanctuary and walked swiftly to the front doors of the church. A woman stumbled into view. She clutched her right hand with the left. The pastor recognized her as a young mother from the congregation.

Pat opened one of the double doors. "Rose?"

"Help me," she whimpered.

"Of course, but come to my office. There are some others, in the sanctuary. They may not want you inside the building. This way." He led her down a long hall and into a small and sparsely decorated room.

"Who did this to you?" the pastor queried after he'd finished dressing the wound.

"My little girl," Rose cried.

"Where is she?" he asked gently as he handed her a cup of water.

"Out in the car, still strapped into her car seat," Rose replied with little care in her voice. Pat moved to leave but Rose grabbed his arm. "Don't let her out. She hasn't been normal since day care."

"We cannot abandon your child, Rose. We should at least bring her inside. *All* are welcome in God's house."

"She isn't my child anymore and God isn't here," Rose cried. Her body had begun to shiver and her teeth chattered uncontrollably.

"You're freezing! I'll get a blanket. Stay here." Pat found a shawl in the lost and found box and headed back to his office. Before he reached the door, Rose appeared in the hallway, pale and uncoordinated.

"You should sit back down," Pat suggested. "I've brought you a shawl."

Rather than listening, Rose ran at him and knocked him to the carpet. She lunged at his face, snapping her teeth like a piranha. Instinctively, he brought his hands up to shield his face but Rose simply bit them instead. He found strength to push her sideways into the secretarial office and with bloody hands he pulled the door closed.

"Ah!" Pat seethed in pain. His hands were covered in tiny holes from Rose's teeth. He put his arms above his head in an attempt to slow the bleeding but it only sent rivulets of blood running down his arms. Rose screamed wildly on the other side of the office door, reminding him that he needed to find safety. He returned to the sanctuary to get aid from the others.

"Stay back, Pat and tell us where you got those wounds," Lila said, backing cautiously away from him.

Pat continued walking.

"Don't come any closer! We've seen some crazy stuff today and it always seems to start with an injury," one of the men warned as he reached for the large bible on the altar. "I don't want to hurt you."

"I'm...already...hur-" Pat managed before collapsing on the carpet.

"He's infected!" Lila screamed. She grabbed the large cross from the wall at the front of the sanctuary. Gripping it like a batter ready to swing, she inched toward the fallen man. "We have to kill him!"

"We can't kill the pastor! He's a man of God! We are God's people!" a woman screamed.

The man with the bible was unconvinced and so swung it high in the air and brought the holy text to a sudden stop against the pastor's head.

"That isn't going to stop him!" Lila yelled as she ran forward, holding the cross at her hip like a jousting stick. The tip of it was sharp and she drove it into his head repeatedly until she was satisfied that he wouldn't be getting back up.

The mini congregation stood in shock. Lila dropped the bloody cross on the carpet and wiped her hands clean on her athletic pants.

"What?" she screamed at them. "It was HIM or us!"

"This doesn't solve the greater problem," the man holding the bible said. "Whoever did this to him is still inside the church!"

"We aren't staying here to find them. This place isn't safe or holy anymore. We'll take the pastor to the morgue and then we should leave town," Lila said confidently as though she'd been planning it for months.

Michelle Kilmer and Rebecca Hansen

A WAY OUT

He thought about it constantly. How he would do it, if he even could? What would his family think when it finally happened? His imminent suicide was all consuming, like death itself would be.

Even though he wanted to die, Cole couldn't use a gun. His father died in a hunting accident when he was 16, leaving his mother, sister and him alone and terrified of anything with a trigger. His gag reflex wouldn't allow a handful of pills to run their course, and wrist cutting seemed too teen-angsty.

The most important reason why traditional suicide methods wouldn't work for him came down to the simple fact that they were *obviously* suicide, death by choice. And he wouldn't do that to his family. He hated himself, but not them.

The plague offered him a solution to both issues. Get sick, get crazy, and get killed. His family, if they survived, would count him as a casualty of chaos, not suicide.

The first reports were from Europe. No one thought it would reach North America, but Cole prayed for it to hitch a ride and find him. When he heard about the San Juan incident he knew his time had come. Now he only had to wait a tiny bit longer.

He spent the day avoiding phone calls from worried family and staring out his living room window for the first signs of disaster. Even though it was his "deathday" he still made a sandwich for lunch and took a midday shower.

"Why am I still inside?" he asked himself as the afternoon wore on. He looked around his rental house one final time, took off his jacket to expose his arms and walked out into the street, not bothering to close the front door.

Cole's first opportunity to die was right in front of him in the house across the street. Through the window he could see his neighbor Evelyn stumbling around the living room chasing after her cat. Looking closer, he could see that clumps of fur lay on the carpet, a sign that the cat had had a few close calls. He went to the front door and tried the knob. Finding it unlocked, he opened it with a *squeak*.

The cat shot into the hallway and ran out the door and down the street. The infected old woman followed closely behind the feline and continued after it, not paying any notice to Cole. He'd missed his chance.

"Shit!" Cole punched the metal mailbox attached to the house. It hurt like hell and he rubbed his knuckles for a moment while he pondered a new death. He wanted to go somewhere he knew would be a mess, like the hospital or the mall, but he might as well write a suicide note for the stupidity that suggested. The only place he could think to go next was his father's grave at the cemetery. He began the long walk up Meridian Avenue, watching for any chance to die that might present itself.

To his right, the freeway was jammed with car after car of commuters-turned-refugees seeking safety outside the city. When he had almost reached the long road that ran through Northgate, he felt a bullet whiz uncomfortably close to his head.

"What the fuck are you doing, kid?" a man's deep and arrogant voice called out to Cole.

Cole looked in the direction of the gun blast and then wished that he hadn't. The man who'd fired on him was tall, muscular, and covered in guns.

"I mean you're just waltzing along out here like the world isn't coming to an end," the man bellowed back as he holstered his handgun.

"Isn't that what you're doing?" Cole retorted.

"Yes, but I'm waltzing with weapons," the man answered as he pointed at his guns.

"Why'd you shoot at me?" Cole asked as he checked his ear for damage.

"I didn't. I shot the leader of your fan club. She was about to get you," the man said as he pointed behind Cole.

Cole turned to see that ten of the infected were nearly upon him. The eleventh was on the pavement with a bullet wound to the head. "What are you, some kind of zombie messiah?"

"Sure. I'll just have to hurry up and die then, right? To resurrect and lead them?" Cole said sarcastically.

"I wouldn't go that far, but suit yourself," the man shrugged and climbed up the fire escape on an apartment building to the left.

Cole moved forward once more. He thought about stopping and letting his "fan club" become one with him but he didn't want to be torn to pieces. He wanted a dignified, clean, one bite transaction. Also, he knew the man was still watching him from his third floor apartment, most likely through a rifle scope.

At his father's gravestone, Cole sat and picked at the grass for a while. Maybe he didn't want to die? Why hadn't he chased after the old woman until she sunk her teeth into him? Or piss off the gun nut until he emptied clip after clip into Cole's world-weary body? Suddenly he missed his mother and wanted nothing more than to see her. He dug his cellphone out of his pocket, saw he'd missed twenty calls from her and then dialed her number from memory.

The phone went straight to voicemail and he heard his mother's voice as expected but the message had been changed.

"Cole, Cole I love you. I've been trying to call you for hours. Your sister was attacked at the University and she…well…she died honey. They want me to view her body but the house is surrounded by sick people and…I can't. I just can't. I'm turning the ringer off and I don't want you to come here for me. I'll be gone, back with your sister and your father. I love you, baby. I'm sorry." The recorded message ended and he left a short one in response.

"I love you too, Mom," he recorded as he pushed himself up from the ground using his father's gravestone for support. At the gate to the cemetery stood a single "sick person", as his mother had called them. Cole walked slowly in its direction, breathing the fall air in as deeply as he could for the last time. He reached the woman and she reached out to him in want.

Cole lifted an arm and offered it to her. She chewed softly at first but when her teeth finally broke his skin and she tasted his muscle and blood, an unnatural hunger took over. Cole relished the pain and the numbness that followed.

It was everything he wanted his death to be.

Michelle Kilmer and Rebecca Hansen

SKIPPING TOWN

No one wanted a body in their car, but after finding the keys to Rose's minivan in the church office the group was able to dispose of the pastor's body. They were now driving aimlessly around the dying town. Serah, Rose's daughter, was still strapped into her car seat and growing more vicious by the minute.

"What the hell do we do now?" one of the church members screamed from the front passenger seat of the vehicle.

"I will *not* have that language in here!" Lila screamed.

"We just killed a man of God and dumped his body! There is a tiny demon strapped between us! We are going to

Hell so what does it matter if I say it? Hell, shit, damn, fuck!" the man bellowed.

"Can someone shut him up? I'm going to lose it!" Lila yelled.

"You killed the pastor, Lila. I think you've already lost it!" a man named Byron said.

Serah's body surged forward, testing the strength of the car seat straps and making the passengers on either side of her jump.

"The more we yell the more excited the demon child becomes!" Byron's wife, Leslie, pointed out. "Everyone just relax."

"Relax?" Lila scoffed. "I have a feeling it's going to be a long time before we can relax.

"I have a gun," a worshipper named John announced.

"And what do you suggest we do with a gun, John? We are not one of those churches! We will not end in mass suicide!" Lila shrieked, appalled at the idea.

"I'd hardly call twelve people 'mass'. And I was suggesting we kill the child," John pointed at the raging little girl.

"We kill one man and now you want to slaughter anyone that irks you?" Lila questioned.

"She wants to kill us and that was *your* justification for killing Pastor Houlihan, Lila. Don't get all 'holier than thou' on me," John said.

"No, no, no, no. There's no way I'm getting into Heaven with the murder of an innocent on my hands," Lila said as she shook her head.

"Fine, can we cover her up then?" John asked.

"No, we cannot. God is watching!" Lila said firmly. She drove the van to a freeway entrance but they couldn't make it far before they hit gridlock. There was no movement for a half hour and Serah growled from the car seat the entire time.

"That is IT! I can't handle this anymore! Can we put her outside?" John asked.

"I like that idea," a woman in the back seat said.

"Just set her loose like a wild animal? No one would look after her," Leslie said.

"I'm pretty sure she can fend for herself!" John shifted uncomfortably in his seat.

"She might kill someone else," Byron said.

"But not us," Lila smiled.

"Your morals are all mixed up, Lila," John said.

"I'm on your side, John. Just put the jacket over her face, unbuckle the straps and grip her as tight as you can! Byron, you get ready to open the door!" she directed.

They did as they were told but Serah broke free of the churchman's grip and jumped onto Byron's lap before he could open the van's large sliding door. She wrapped her arms tightly around his head and sunk her teeth into his face. He attempted to pry the child from his body but she clung to him. When he finally succeeded in pulling her away she took one of his eyeballs with her.

"Aaaaaah!" he cried out. Others in the van started screaming along with him. Lila jumped out and closed the driver's side door behind her. Serah chewed on the meaty sphere with an unintentional smacking of her lips. John pulled his gun and aimed it at the child as she leaned in for Byron's other eye. John followed her with the gun, closed his eyes and pulled the trigger. The bullet exploded from the barrel and into the side of Byron's head, effectively silencing him and ending his misery.

"You killed Byron!" Leslie shrieked. Throwing her purse at John's head. Serah pulled Byron's other eye from its socket, giving the rest of the group time to flee the van. Everyone left but Leslie, who was trying to strangle Serah.

"He had beautiful eyes and you ATE them!!! What is wrong with you?" Leslie shook the little girl but it did nothing to dissuade her. The moment she let go of the girl's neck, Serah attacked her just as she had Byron.

Outside, Lila and the remainder of the group traveled north on foot, away from the city. John kept his gun un-holstered; Lila kept her bible in hand. Many other uninfected people from the traffic jam walked with them but the sick were growing in number, making the journey dangerous.

Lila read as they walked, "For I am sure that neither death nor life, nor angels nor rulers, nor things present nor things to come, nor powers, nor height nor depth, nor anything else in all creation, will be able to separate us from the love of God in Christ Jesus our Lord."

HOLED UP

"Your papers are in order, Ms. Kruse. You've got unit number 35. I'll show you how to open the gate and then you'll want to follow the road down the middle and turn right at the end of the row. It's the space on the corner."

"Ok, great. I have my stuff out in the truck. Can I move it in today?" Miranda pointed over her shoulder to the Dodge in the parking lot.

"Yeah, no problem," the man at the rental desk replied.

Miranda followed him outside. She hopped in her truck and, with the window down, pulled to the gate where the man waited for her.

"Here's your entry code," he said as he handed her a printed scrap of paper. "Press the pound key and then the code and it'll open. You can come 24 hours a day but the office is only open until five-thirty on weekdays."

She leaned out the window and typed the code as he directed, the gate slid open.

"On the first try!" the man exclaimed. "I'm impressed."

Miranda laughed and drove the truck to the storage space marked '35'. It was small for the price she was paying but it was necessary. She was leaving the state for three months for a well-deserved vacation. "Arizona, here I come." Miranda daydreamed about the dry climate and the guaranteed good weather of the southern state as she unloaded the twenty or so boxes from the truck bed.

After half an hour, the site manager came by to check on her progress. "Hi Ms. Kruse, looks like you're almost done here."

"Only a few more boxes and then I'm heading out!" she smiled.

"Well, the office is closed but if you really need me I live on-site in that house over there," the man pointed to a small building that was half inside and half outside of the gate. "And my name is Alan."

"Oh, ok." Miranda thought it a strange piece of information to give. He must be hitting on her.

"Have a good day!" the storage manager waved and made his way to his rambler.

The last boxes stacked tidily in the glorified locker, Miranda pulled the metal door down and secured it with a heavy-duty lock. She drove her truck to the gate but found she couldn't leave without her access code, which she couldn't find.

"Uuuugh!" she screamed in frustration as she looked around the cab for the piece of paper that the manager had given her. Out the windshield she could see the manager walking away from her on the other side of the gate. Miranda put the truck in park and got out to call to him, "Excuse me!" she yelled. The man turned in her direction and roared animalistically.

"Oh my god!" she shrieked. His face and arms were smeared with blood and he staggered as though he was intoxicated. "What happened to you?"

Alan continued toward Miranda even when the gate blocked him from reaching her. He struggled against the metal barrier, transferring blood from his body to its surface. Across the street from the storage facility, she could see that other people were behaving the same way.

Miranda returned to her truck. *Is it some kind of zombie walk?* She wondered. It looked so real.

The manager still bumped against the gate. He didn't seem to recognize her. She put the truck into reverse and backed slowly into the depths of the storage rows. Even if she found her gate code, she wasn't sure that opening it was a good idea. Miranda found a spot to turn around inside the facility. She drove through every row and around the entire perimeter, checking to make sure she was alone.

Once more she put the truck in park but this time she killed the engine. She had time to collect her thoughts, right?

No one was waiting for her in Arizona and Miranda had left her job four days before. Her old apartment was empty and had been cleaned for the next tenant. Her cellphone sat on the passenger seat to her right. It chimed a special ring she'd set for her father, and so she answered it.

"Hi, Dad," she said, now aware that her heart was pounding anxiously in her chest. She could hear breathing on the other end but he didn't respond. "Hello?"

"One of those things, it got me pretty bad on the shoulder. I need you to get help for me, can you do that?" He finished and moaned loudly in pain.

"I'm stuck at the storage place on 99. What's going on?"

"Maybe I can help myself. Look, honey, don't go to Arizona. You should probably just stay put until help comes."

"Help? What do you mean, help? The manager is outside of the gate and he is covered in blood. I'm the only person in here!"

"Stay in your truck and lock the doors. Do you have a blanket or any food?"

"You're scaring me, Dad."

The phone call disconnected.

"Dad?" she screamed. She dialed his number but he didn't answer. Now desperate to get out to help her father, she returned to her storage unit to look for the gate code. The small slip of paper was on the ground next to the metal door of her space.

"Oh thank God," she said as she climbed back into the truck but her happiness was short-lived. A woman, missing an arm and with blood still dripping from the severed end, shuffled around the corner at the end of the row. Miranda felt a tear fall from her eye, the fear slowly building within her. She got in the cab and locked the door. More people followed behind the woman, each with their own set of disturbing wounds. Somehow the monsters had gotten in.

They surrounded her truck and pounded on the frame; demanding entry. Miranda screamed aloud. A terror unlike anything she'd felt before filled her gut. She needed to get out but there was no way she would stick her arm out of the window to punch in the gate code, not with the dangerous people out there. The engine of the truck turned over smoothly and she drove through the crowd of bloodied people toward the front of the complex. Seeing that the gate was indeed still closed, she parked the truck alongside the low roof of the manager's on-site house and prepared to climb out the small back window into the truck bed. Just as she was sticking an arm through, her cellphone rang again. This time the word "Mom" was displayed on the screen. Miranda sat back down in the cab and answered it.

"Hello?" she said desperately, expecting the same strained and worrisome response her father had given.

"Oh, good girl, you're ok!" her mother said with relief. "I can't get a hold of your father and there's something strange going on outside. Are you somewhere safe?"

"Well, I was working on that when you called. I'm going to climb on a roof for the time being. Where are you?"

"I'm in the attic at home. Someone broke in through the big glass window in the front room so I had to run up here."

"There's nothing to eat up there!" Miranda worried but then realized she was in the same predicament.

"I didn't have a choice, hun. Have you heard from your father?"

Miranda didn't want to tell her that she had spoken to him and that he was injured so she lied, "No, no I haven't."

"I'll have to try again. Listen, call me later if you can. Love you!" her mother said before hanging up.

With her jacket and purse stuffed out the rear window, she squeezed her body through. The angry and disoriented people had once again surrounded the truck and were reaching their arms across the sides of the bed to grab her. She was thankful that her hair was short as it was one less thing for them to get a hold of. From the truck bed she climbed on top of the cab and then it was a small step up onto the roof of the one-story house. Now safe from clawing hands, Miranda took a moment to catch her breath.

"I fucking hate this place," she said as she looked out on the dying city. Below her the infected gathered in increasing numbers, reducing her chances of ever getting out.

DEADLINE

Thump!

A large furry body crashed on top of Timothy Kubiak as he napped on the couch. It was Tuesday afternoon, and as usual his golden retriever was his personal alarm clock.

lick *lick* *lick*

Cheddar's large, sloppy tongue founds its way up Timothy's cheek and over his left eye.

"Stop it, Cheddar," Timothy whispered, "I'm not ready to get back to work quite..."

Thwack!

One of Cheddar's oversized paws landed directly on Timothy's mouth causing an abrupt end to the sentence.

"Ok, ok, I'm up," Timothy laughed as he pet the dog's head. Cheddar lifted his paw for a handshake. "Food first, handshakes later, buddy."

Timothy's job as an illustrator allowed him to work from home, make his own schedule, spend a lot of time with his dog and nap in the middle of the day. He pulled sweatpants on over his boxer shorts and made his way to the kitchen, four furry legs followed closely behind.

"Ok, Mr. Kubiak, what do we want to snack on?" Timothy asked the dog as he opened up the pantry. "Looks like kibble for you and an apple for me."

With Cheddar temporarily distracted by a fresh bowl of food, he took his snack to the living room and turned on the news.

"Our top story today is the ineffective quarantine of two major San Juan islands. Officials aren't providing many details, but highly recommend staying indoors and away from anyone who appears sick or disoriented. Stay tuned for continuing coverage on what we're hoping is not an epidemic. I'm Eva Cassinelli with News Five."

"Eeewww, sounds nasty!" Timothy said, his voice automatically summoning Cheddar to his side. "Let's try to get some work done. What do you say, boy?" Cheddar gave him a front paw to shake as if to say 'It's a deal'. "Alright then Mr. Kubiak, let's go," he said as he shook the dog's paw. Turning off the TV, he left the living room and entered his home office to start the days' work. He turned his computer on and his cellphone off to cut down on distractions.

Laid out before him on his desk were sheets of paper covered in logo ideas for a deadline at the end of the week, but inspiration had still not struck him. For an hour he randomly sketched shapes but nothing jumped off of the page. Cheddar was no help, coming in and out of the office at random intervals, sometimes with a bone in his mouth and other times just for another paw shake.

Once more, the dog came into the room, but instead of bothering Timothy he ran to one of the windows and stood up to its sill. Never one to make much noise it was more than concerning when Cheddar started to growl.

"Cheddar? What's wrong?" Timothy went to the window and looked outside to see what had aggravated his dog. A man he recognized as a neighbor ran quickly by the window, through the side yard. "We know him, boy, get off the wall," he stroked Cheddar's head and coaxed him to the floor. Back at the desk, his dog wouldn't leave his side. The paw-giving was increased tenfold as though it were a nervous tick. When Cheddar's restless paw pulled some of the drawings to the floor, Timothy lost his patience and swatted it away.

"Unless that paw of yours can draw, it's useless here! Out!" he yelled, pointing to the office door. Cheddar did as he was told and wandered to another part of the house. Left with his frustration, Timothy realized he wouldn't be able to create anything great without first clearing his head. He looked to the bicycle-shaped paperweight on his desk and decided a bike ride was just what he needed.

He changed out of his house clothes and into biking attire, a full body spandex number that showed off his tight butt and well-developed calf muscles. Cheddar stared at him as he tied the laces of his biking shoes, occasionally bopping Timothy's legs with his paw. "Not this time, puppers. I'm riding solo."

Kenneling Cheddar, Timothy left through his garage and started biking up the street. His route of choice for the day took him toward the hospital, some 25 blocks north and then back south again. Ambulances flew by him several times and cars darted dangerously around him in a manner more hurried than usual. A minivan turned a corner in front of him, its brakes screeching wildly.

"Share the road!" Timothy yelled. He hopped the curb into a patch of grass to rest a moment. Through the hedge in front of him he could see gravestones. *Creepy,* he thought. Up the road a horn honked and a loud crash of metal on metal rang out. The minivan that had almost hit him had collided with another vehicle in front of the hospital. Timothy considered helping the motorists but after his near death experience with the minivan, he decided they deserved the accident.

Riding back home, the world was a chaotic blur. He was shaken from the close call with the van and eager to get back to his desk to put some new ideas on paper. At the ten-block mark he saw a green light ahead and so, pushed his feet hard into the pedals. Traveling at top speed from east to west toward the same intersection, a woman in a black Suburban wasn't paying attention to the red light begging her to stop. The impact was brutal, sending Timothy and his bike flying west down the road where the SUV hit him again, this time running over his already destroyed body before coming to a stop.

His lifeless form lie on the road contorted and ripped open. Intestines trailed behind a back tire of the SUV.

ABOUT THE AUTHORS

MICHELLE KILMER

The Spread is Michelle Kilmer's second book. She is also the author of When the Dead. She currently lives in a secured-access apartment in Seattle, WA with her husband, a machete and a fear of the dark.

REBECCA HANSEN

Rebecca is twin sister to Michelle and lover of everything zombie. The Spread is her first contribution to the genre.

When she isn't plotting gruesome fictional deaths she fancies hiking, painting and watching low budget and foreign horror movies. A seasoned special effects make-up artist, she turns willing subjects into the walking dead on the weekends.

She lives just north of Seattle with her boyfriend, three attack cats, a gun, axe, machete and small collection of knives.

KEEP FOLLOWING THE PLAGUE

It doesn't end here! Check out Michelle Kilmer's When the Dead to find out what happens next. Turn the page to read an excerpt!

Have you ever wondered what might happen if a group of survivors decided to stay put? To never leave the safety of home to search for salvation? When the Dead . . . provides one scenario to answer the question. In a world where neighbors are strangers and we live behind locked doors, the living dead can really bring issues to a head.

There is no way out for the residents of Willow Brook Apartments. Outside a plague is spreading while behind the walls, neighbors are forced to become friends . . . or enemies. When the Dead . . . will introduce you to a doomed family, a dying child, an egomaniac, a murderer, and other undesirables (including the undead!!) in three floors of secured-access chaos.

"Engaging and terrifying" - "a story about people under pressure" - "More than a zombie story. When the Dead speaks to the human spirit and lack thereof." - "...will haunt your thoughts for sometime to come"

WHEN THE DEAD

(excerpt)

THE INFECTION

It starts with a cold sweat then a swift drop in body temperature that makes the teeth chatter. The skin feels itchy and hot but the insides are dying from the cold.

Then the numbness starts in the extremities. Finger tips, toes, up through the feet and hands into the legs and arms and finally the core. It cannot be rubbed out as the hands do not work anymore.

It reaches the chest and the ability to control the breathing is lost. Just before the last breath of air escapes the lungs, numbness reaches the head.

The eyes go crazy, the tongue limp. One cannot call out for help as the head falls on the chest. There is but a single moment for the dying self to think a final thought . . .

Why me?
But then . . . you aren't you anymore.

Michelle Kilmer

Fucked

"I can't understand what they're saying," Edward said as he slammed a fist down on the radio.

"You could try another station. That sounds like French they're speaking," his wife Moira suggested. She had wanted a television for a long time but Edward preferred the way the voices came floating from the speakers into the apartment. This meant that in the current situation though, they had to rely on the radio show hosts' graphic descriptions to give them any idea of what was going on in cities across the globe.

"The other stations keep replaying the same stuff. It's not getting any better; only worse," Edward grumbled.

"Then there's nothing we can do but make some tea and wait to see what happens next."

"It's happening everywhere," Isobel said to her mother over the phone. She had spent the morning reading news articles online. She had watched a clip of someone succumb to the infection on a CDC table, surrounded by plastic and strapped down like a criminal or lunatic.

"Things will be ok, Isobel! They have a carrier. It really is only a matter of time. If they can study it, they can find a cure or at least a vaccine. Try to keep this thing from spreading any further."

"It's too big already. The world is fucked. I've got to go." She hung up the phone not knowing it would be the last time she'd speak to her mother.

"On and on for three days, man; can't they talk about something else?" Vaughn turned off his television angrily. "Could have been aliens, maybe the government, maybe bio-terrorists? Shut up." He chucked a drained beer can at the black screen. "Just fix it and forget it!"

Vaughn was alone, as he often was, unless he paid for company. He was talking to himself. He probably couldn't even pay someone to listen to him. Especially when he was drunk and that was most of the time.

"Couldn't be bio-terrorists, they'd a laid claim to it. Been proud of the trouble they were causing. Pretty fancy stuff making dead people come back to life. It has to be the government; only group with enough funding and closed doors to pull this shit off."

The infection was quickly spreading. It had reached terrorist groups and government groups alike. It lay in thousands of sickbeds, it rode the bus, and it lived next door to many already. No one was immune from this unstoppable plague.

the infection does not discriminate in human hosts. sex, race and religious conviction no longer divide the population.

The number one cause for the spread of the disease was denial. It made no *sense* to anyone. News media could be blamed for the lies with headlines like *It's impossible! Death is death, the final breath,* and *People Don't Come Back. They stay wherever it is that they went.*

Michelle Kilmer

WILLOW BROOK APARTMENTS

Willow Brook is a three-story building, four if you count the basement. Each floor has six two-bedroom apartments with identical floor plans.

The kitchen is to the left of the entry. It has an island that looks out on the dining room and living room. The first room on the right down the hallway is a second bedroom. Next is the laundry closet with a stacking washer/dryer unit. The last room on the right is the bathroom. At the end of the hall is a closet and the master bedroom is on the left.

All of the apartments look more or less like this save for differences in décor and varying levels of tidiness. The Willow Brook building is controlled access, meaning that if you don't have a key, someone has to buzz you in, or not.

Michelle Kilmer

THE FIRST DAY

On the morning of the first day, the day that things would start to change for the residents of Willow Brook Apartments, things looked normal. When Isobel Shiffman looked outside it was almost too normal, right down to the happy thieving squirrel in the tree nearest her living room window.

Northgate is at the northern edge of Seattle and the nearest reports of the disease were further north in Everett and south in Tacoma, still far enough away for Isobel to brave the outdoors. Her mother had told her to stock up on food just in case things didn't clear up as quickly as she hoped. Isobel had gone shopping on Sunday and it was only Tuesday but her mother insisted.

Like Isobel, the rest of the city driven by nagging mothers, packed into the grocery stores and left them in such a state of disarray that it was hard for her to navigate. The cart, even without the help of the wobbly right front wheel, kept running into things: cans of food, a bag of chips, some nylons, and other items strewn about. All of which were displaced far from their original aisle and shelf. She struggled with it until she found the secret to making the cart move was to put pressure on the left side of it with her foot. She went for some of the fresh food that everyone else was ignoring, figuring it could be eaten first and when it ran out or started to rot, whichever happened first, she'd break into the non-perishables (of which she had a lot).

She made it up to the only open checkout lane.

"How long did you buy for?" the nervous cashier asked.

"Um . . . I don't know. A week?" Isobel wasn't good at estimation or small talk. Her cart was full with what she knew was affordable for her budget and, more importantly, what she could carry up to her second floor apartment on her own. She hadn't been thinking about timelines.

"That won't be enough. The world is coming to an end."

"Ok. Well how long do you buy for when the world is coming to an end?" Isobel snapped at the cashier.

"Don't know," the cashier shrugged. "Do you want your receipt?"

"Sure."

On the way back home, the radio still reporting news from all over, documented the plague's movement. It crept slowly closer. Isobel turned the radio up and listened.

"Early this morning, a ferry full of people trying to get home to their families left Whidbey Island alive and well and arrived at the Edmonds ferry dock infected with the mysterious disease we've been seeing. They had somehow contracted the disease on the passage over the Puget Sound. Ferry officials at the Edmonds Pier heard no reports from the captain of the vessel that anything was wrong on the boat. The captain routinely steered the ship into port and the infected disembarked and started attacking people in the parking lot. It is suspected that at least twenty of the infected passengers made it out of the ferry terminal and into downtown Edmonds. Efforts to locate and apprehend them in order to contain the spread of the infection have been unsuccessful. Several injured passengers made it safely onto lifeboats before the ferry made it ashore, but they did not survive their wounds. The captain of the vessel has been detained for questioning at this time."

The program switched to weather and Isobel changed the station, desperate to find out just how close it had become.

"- determined that the perpetrator of a street fight in downtown Seattle, described by witnesses as a "drunken transient", was actually a person suffering from the infection. Police shot the man after he attempted to attack them. It is unknown how he came into contact with the disease. Attempts to identify the individual are ongoing, as his body appeared to be in a state of decomposition. The flesh of his fingertips was gone, rendering fingerprinting useless. Investigators are working with dental records -"

Isobel changed it again, looking for another news story and its location.

"A group of students started a riot on University Avenue in the U-District just after eleven a.m. Over fifty college students were injured in the event, four fatally. The group seemed to have no agenda and was only intent on causing destruction and harm to individuals. Sources at the scene noted that the group was not involved in looting or property damage. Most of the students fled the scene before they could be arrested and interrogated. Campus police had great difficulty dealing with the problem and are not commenting at this time. It is still unknown whether the perpetrators were rioting in response to the disease, or as a result of being infected with it."

Isobel's heart beat faster.

"A bloody scene at the Helene Madison Pool greeted Shoreline Police investigators midday today. A lifeguard interviewed said that a man had emerged from the men's locker room at the start of Public Swim and started attacking children in the shallow end of the pool. It took two lifeguards on staff to remove the man from the water and hold him while a third employee called the police. All of the children involved suffered only minor injuries. The pool has been shut down for investigation and sanitation reasons and will remain closed until further notice."

"That's just up the road," she said to herself.

Initial reports thought the disease spread and made people psychotic and violent; that the infected were living people with altered minds and an inability to differentiate right from wrong. Whatever the process, it only took one infected person to ruin everybody's day.

Approaching from all directions, the disease was soon upon Isobel's neighborhood and suddenly it was right in front of her in the form of a traffic accident. Someone had destroyed a bicyclist with an SUV. A deep cut in his abdomen sat open, displaying his intestines. One of his legs had been almost completely severed near the hip joint. He had not survived his injuries. The driver of the vehicle, a pale young woman in hysterics and leggings, was leaning over the dead man when he sat back up, guts spilling from his body, and bit her face, taking a chunk out of her cheek as she screamed for help. Isobel wasn't the only driver that swerved around the mess. She could still hear the woman's yelling as she sped the last three blocks home. *There was nothing I could do to help the man or the woman,* she thought over and over again, trying to calm her nerves and her conscience. The world was feeling much smaller to her; the troubles of it more her own now.

She pulled her car into the parking lot of Willow Brook and quickly lugged her two bags of groceries from the lot to the front door.

"Whroah roah wrooah! Roah!" A giant black poodle jumped into her making her scream and drop her food.

"Kiki, no! Get down! Bad dog, BAD DOG!" Sheila Brown from apartment 201 yelled, tugging roughly on her dog's leash and dragging it up the stairs.

"Oh, it's ok. I can pick it all up myself. Really, don't worry about it!" Isobel said to Sheila who was already out of earshot. "Thanks for the apology too, bitch."

Upstairs she put the groceries away with what was already in the cupboards. Her food situation looked much better to her now so for the rest of the first day she sat alone in the living room in front of the television, eyes glued to news report after bloody news report; ears listening intently to the speculation. Several times she hopped up to check that the door was locked. She was still having trouble mentally digesting what she'd seen on the road earlier. *Maybe the bicyclist wasn't dead? Perhaps he was just knocked unconscious and when he came to, in all his pain and bewilderment, he lashed out?* No story she made up explained how the man could be alive after suffering wounds so horrific, nor why he would want to bite the driver who shattered and shredded his body.

His guts were on the road, she kept coming back to this single sight, this undeniable fact. No one sits up with his guts on the road.

S.O.S.-LESS

Many people still had a very strong sense that things would be ok because they had no contact with the disease yet. They were viewing the plague on televisions and computer screens, not in person. Their faith in the police force, that the uniformed men and women in affected areas could get things under control, was strong. Stronger still was the idea that all of the world's best scientists would be gathering in a sterile room at an undisclosed location, working day and night until they found the cause and then the cure. Hollywood had showed the citizens this response so this is what they demanded; what their minds had decided would happen - *was* happening. The population waited for quarantines and white-suited specialists with giant mobile labs but they didn't come. Many CDC labs had already been overrun with the dead.

As the day disappeared and night came, things were falling apart fast as the spread of the infection continued from one complacent and unprepared house to another. In Northgate strange noises filled the air, mixed with relentless emergency response sirens. Isobel turned off the television, filled the bathtub with water just in case it stopped running, cooked some pork chops and drowned out the horrible cacophony with her mp3 player.

Slowly she fell asleep. Around one in the morning the gunshots picked up and tore her from her rest. Unable to regain unconsciousness over the noise, Isobel turned the television back on. The dead weren't just coming back;

they were definitely coming back hungry. Her mind returned to the bicyclist. *He wasn't lashing out in anger; he was trying to bite her!* The confirmation was terrifying. The attacks had spread so quickly that the infection had reached uncontainable levels. With one eye open, Isobel barely slept at all the rest of the first night.

END OF EXCERPT!

Grab a copy today! When the Dead is available in paperback and e-book from Amazon.com.

Made in the USA
San Bernardino, CA
22 February 2014